Braiding Fortunes: A Story of Luck and Bravery of the Heart

Act I – Fortune Woven

Braiding Fortunes: A Story of Luck and Bravery of the Heart

Act I – Fortune Woven

J. A. Springs

WRITING
FOR THE
WORLD
PRESS
since
2021

Lancaster, PA. 17603

ISBNs 13:
978-1-966464-19-8 (eBook)
978-1-966464-20-4 (Paperback)

Dedication

To those who know—
love isn't always messy between hearts,
but in the noise that surrounds them.

Author's Note

This story began, as some do, with a song.

Chris Stapleton's *Starting Over* came on one restless afternoon, and a single line stopped me.

That lyric lodged in my chest.

Not because it promised escape, but because it promised *presence*—a choice to be with someone despite the chaos around you.

Not for comfort. Not for safety.

But for love.

That idea stayed with me.

And from it, two characters emerged:

– A boy of mixed heritage, noble in spirit, unshaken by the weight of history.

– A girl of English birth, full of quiet rebellion and louder grace.

I set their story in the late 1700s because I didn't need to *add* obstacles to make their love story hard.

The world had already written those into the record.

They meet in a time of colonial unrest, religious divide, and racial brutality.

And still, they fall into something tender. Something risky. Something neither of them fully understands—until it's too late to pretend otherwise.

I named them Penny and Clauvère for a reason.

One a symbol of chance.

The other of luck.

This is their gamble.

And if you're willing to take that chance with them,

you just might find a piece of yourself braided into their fortune.

—*J. A. Springs*

PART ONE

Penelope and Clauvère
In their youth

1

In the year 1770, the sun hung low in the Southern sky, casting a golden glow over the bustling port of Savannah, Georgia. Clauvère Jean-Claude de La Pointierre, a twelve-year-old boy, and his mother, Minuette Notette de La Pointierre, disembarked from their ship, their hearts filled with both anticipation and anxiety. The salty breeze rustled the hems of Clauvère's coat as he stood upon the busied waterfront, his eyes wide with curiosity.

Clauvère was a mulatto, his skin bearing the warm hues of his mixed West Indian heritage. He had arrived in this strange new land with his mother, Minuette, who shared his mixed ancestry. Her deep brown eyes scanned the busy docks. They were free persons of color, newly arrived in this turbulent city.

Clauvère's father, Chevalier Louis Jean-Baptiste de La Pointierre, a white Frenchman of dashing countenance, had arrived in Savannah weeks before them. He oversaw the family sugar plantation in the French West Indies, but he had come to the American colonies before them with a specific purpose. His goal was to establish a sugar trade through George Hartford, a colonial businessman based in Savannah. He had even purchased a quaint yet elegant home for his family in this new world, a place where he intended to introduce his son to the intricacies of colonial life and expand his worldly views and understanding.

Louis was a man of ambition, looking to solidify his partnership with George. His business ventures, however, had left Clauvère and Minuette to explore Savannah while they waited for him to come and retrieve them upon their arrival.

They were a family divided less by comprehension than by choice. Clauvère, fluent in both French and English, was the bridge between their lineages. Louis had taught him early, knowing that business demanded many tongues. Minuette, though she understood English well enough, rarely spoke it. In Martinique she had called it *la langue rude*—the coarse language—unsuited to her ear and to polite company. She preferred the grace of her native speech and used it exclusively, allowing her son to translate when courtesy required.

"Par où commencer, maman?" (Where do we begin, mother?) Clauvère asked, his voice betraying a touch of uncertainty.

Minuette's face softened as she looked down at her son. "Nous commençons par trouver un endroit où reposer nos pieds fatigués, mon cher. Et peut-être un morceau de nourriture pour nos ventres affamés." (We begin by finding a place to rest our weary feet, my dear. And perhaps a morsel of food for our hungry bellies.)

Minuette gestured off vaguely down the street before them, and indicated that she and her son should head off there, first.

Clauvère stepped onto the cobblestone streets, the warmth of the afternoon sun embracing his skin. He marveled at the quaint streets and pathways that meandered through the city. The town was alive with the energy of commerce.

As they ventured further into the city, the vibrant mix of cultures and languages filled the air. Gullah songs from the docks merged with the brusque timbre of English and the melodic accents of some French Huguenots in the market. Clauvère and Minuette marveled at the mosaic of life in Savannah, a place alive with a mixture of peoples.

As they strolled down a particular bustling street, they encountered curious glances and hushed conversations from the locals. Clauvère translated some of these comments for his mother, but he chose not to share the less welcoming remarks.

His maman, dressed in a manner befitting the free mulattos of the West Indies who patterned their dress after the fashions of the metropole, maintained her dignity, unfazed by the stares. Her attire—French in its cut and refinement, the sort of metropolitan elegance rarely seen among the English commoner populace—only deepened their differences from those around them.

A hoop skirt of fine silk, a corseted bodice, and pearls gathered at her throat, the cameo nestled at her décolletage catching the light—every detail spoke of Parisian grace rather than colonial simplicity. It was French elite culture at its finest, and all the more disquieting to those unaccustomed to seeing such refinement on a woman of her hue.

Clauvère thought it odd that he and his mother should be regarded as they were by many of those passing near them. This had never occurred in Martinique. He couldn't help but feel the pressure of their gazes as the two strolled side by side.

Their journey had brought them to the heart of a place where he had first felt hope for a new experience—but now something else was woven through it, tightly bound and unspoken. Clauvère noticed how their presence seemed to stir a range of emotions in the townsfolk.

They were an unusual sight, a free mixed-race family in a time when such unions were rarely accepted. In the French West Indies, unions between whites and blacks were not common, yet neither were they unheard of and they were generally accepted. He'd seen his fair share of such unions while growing up there. There was a large and expanding population of mixed heritage within Martinique and other cities of the West Indies.

He had never experienced bias like this, however.

The whispered comments startled him first; now the looks were unsettling him more deeply. Many passersby cast curious glances their way, their expressions a mixture of fascination and intrigue. Some had likely never encountered people of mixed heritage before. They would point and whisper among themselves, as if trying to decipher the mystery of their background.

Clauvère overheard a passing woman remark to her companion, "The dress is remarkable but—"

Her voice faltered when her eyes met Clauvère's steady gaze. She hurried away, her companion close behind, as though suddenly reminded of some pressing errand.

Then there were those whose expressions were tainted with shock and awe. They were perhaps taken aback by the elegance and grace with which Minuette carried herself, dressed in her finery, and her son, Clauvère, who bore the demeanor of a well-educated young man who held his head high with assurance.

These onlookers could not readily reconcile their preconceived notions with the reality before them. Many were indifferent. However, it appeared that many others of those they passed by displayed open disapproval. Their frowns, cold glares, and hushed insults hung heavily in the air.

Clauvère's heart ached for his mother, who bore the greater share of these stares, and the brunt of their jaundiced comments. She couldn't understand what they were saying due to her limited command of the language, but he could. He tried to hide the hurt in his eyes while memories of his homeland returned to him—the easier streets of Martinique, where such glances had never followed them.

For a fleeting moment, Clauvère desired for a return to a world where he and his mother could walk the streets without skeptical gazes full of intolerance. Where love and acceptance outweighed suspicion and disdain. But for now, he held his head high and carried the difference that marked both himself and his maman with noble dignity, resolute in his determination to judge it only after time had instructed him. He would do this for the sake of his parents, and for the expectations of noblesse oblige. Still, he longed for a place for himself in a world that he was beginning to learn often refused to accept people who were different.

Clauvère brushed the dark thoughts aside and gave his maman a warm smile when she looked down at him. He sought to alleviate her worries that this change in their lives might have a bad effect upon him. He was, indeed, a bit more mature for his age than people typically ascribed to one so young, so he could see some things in ways that adults could as well.

They soon stumbled upon a lively square where a group of musicians played a spirited tune on fiddles and tambourines. The rhythm was infectious, and Clauvère couldn't help but tap his foot, while Minuette swayed to the music, her eyes twinkling.

They had left behind the days of their previous life, and here in Savannah, they felt the beginnings of a promise of something new. A fragrant breeze carried the scent of fried catfish from a nearby food stall. Minuette led Clauvère to the vendor, her mouth watering slightly. As they savored each crispy bite of fish, they chatted with a few locals who happened to be less reluctant to openly converse with them. These strangers happily shared tales of the city's history.

Their warmth reminded Minuette briefly of home—until, as they crossed into the market square, a man at a nearby stall called out, "Fine fruit from the islands!" Minuette turned, curious.

"Des fruits des îles, Clauvère. Tu veux des fruits?" (Fruits of the islands, Clauvère. Do you want fruit?) she smiled to her son.

The man smiled, holding up a mango, but his expression faltered when he saw her gloved hands and the pearls at her throat—the bronze patina of her skin tone when her flowing hat no longer shaded her face. The light brushed the curve of her cheek and lingered there, the delicate shape of her mouth—a visage so refined it unsettled even admiration itself.

He lowered his gaze and muttered something she couldn't catch. Clauvère caught the man's glance returning, more deliberate this time. The stare lingered—open, unguarded—until Minuette turned her head at a sound in the distance and the merchant's mouth fell slightly ajar.

Clauvère looked up at his mother; the faint sheen upon her skin seemed almost to gather the light about her. When he glanced back at the merchant, the man's expression had shifted: embarrassment rushed to his cheeks as he turned aside in haste while an audible click accompanied the closing of his mouth. Yet something in it unsettled Clauvère—a contradiction he could not name. It was the same quiet spell his mother cast upon the men of Martinique, but here it was laced with something else.

Her attention returning to the moment, she glanced down at her son. "Que?" (What?) she muttered to Clauvère.

"He thought you were buying for someone else," Clauvère lied quietly as he reached up to clasp his maman's hand, his grasp more assertive than it should have been.

"Mais je n'achète que pour moi-même," (But I buy only for myself.) she replied, lifting her chin.

Her finger moved to tap her chin before she smiled down gently at Clauvère, disarming him easily. He found himself blushing as well, feeling the need to turn away from his mother's gaze before softly pulling her away.

They moved on, the air a bit heavier than before. Amidst the colonial backdrop, Clauvère couldn't help but be drawn to the growing tension that was brewing. He sensed the undercurrent of rebellion against the British Crown through snatches of conversations from passerby and wondered how this might affect their lives in this new land.

As they approached a bustling market square, Clauvère spotted a poster, partially concealed in an alley, emblazoned with the bold words of revolution. The contents were lost on his mother, but he understood the fiery language of freedom and defiance. Words like *Freedom, Resistance,* and *Revolution* stood out in bold relief on the yellowing, torn paper.

Clauvère turned to his mother and offered a reassuring smile, "C'est beau ici, n'est-ce pas, Maman?" (It's beautiful here, isn't it, Mother?)

Minuette smiled back, a mother's love transcending language barriers, "Oui, mon fils, c'est magnifique." (Yes, my son, it is magnificent.)

The sun began its descent, casting long shadows across the cobblestone streets. Clauvère and Minuette found a bench, not too far from the docks, nestled beneath the branches of a sprawling live oak tree, its limbs adorned with Spanish moss, and there they rested. They had circled back to where they had started. The city's pulse surrounded them, the hum of conversation and distant laughter forming a soothing backdrop.

"Clauvère," Minuette began, her voice a gentle melody, "Ton père nous trouvera ici. Je le sais dans mon cœur." (Your father will find us here. I know it in my heart.)

Clauvère nodded, his gaze filled with determination. "Oui, mère. Et je serai prêt à l'embrasser." (Yes, Mother. And I will be ready to embrace him.)

It had been unexpected that his father had not been there immediately to retrieve them as they left the ship, but they worried not. He would come, and they would be waiting. Their current place was not that far from where they had disembarked and they could easily be seen from the road leading to the docks.

In that moment, Clauvère and Minuette enjoyed the city of Savannah and all they had experienced of it that day. They waited patiently for the arrival of the man that was the center of their family.

As the golden sun continued its descent beyond the horizon, long shadows stretched across the vibrant port. Not long after they had chosen their resting place, the sound of horses stepping in unison drew Clauvère's attention, and he turned to see the source.

His eyes caught the glittering flash of gold upon the side of a carriage—an insignia set into the polished paneling, the crest of their noble house. Hope stirred immediately in Clauvère's chest that this might be his father approaching them. Looking closer, he saw a familiar figure seated upon the carriage as it trundled along the cobbled streets. Chevalier Thibault, the family retainer, held the reins, driving the team of white horses. The polished wood and gleaming brass of the vehicle caught the fading light as it moved through the lively crowd.

Clauvère's heart quickened as he recognized the dashing countenance of his father, Louis, seated proudly beside the driver.

Clauvère and Minuette rose from the bench beneath the sprawling oak tree as the carriage drew nearer. The air seemed suddenly charged with anticipation. Clauvère could scarcely contain his excitement, and his mother's eyes shone with quiet happiness.

Louis' arrival marked the beginning of a new chapter for the de La Pointierre family. They had journeyed from afar over dangerous waters to this unfamiliar land, and now they were at last reunited.

Clauvère noticed the eyes of onlookers gathering upon them. Their meticulous dress, their mixed heritage, and the white nobleman who had come to collect them presented a sight few in Savannah had likely witnessed before. Curious glances—some fascinated, others uneasy—passed through the watching crowd.

As the carriage came to a graceful halt, Louis stepped down, his gaze first finding his wife and then his son. The distance that had separated them for a time was replaced in that moment with the warmth of homecoming. Tears of joy glistened in Minuette's eyes as she embraced her husband.

"Mon trésor," (My treasure.) Louis whispered as his lips brushed her cheeks.

Clauvère smiled as he watched them. A mixture of slight embarrassment at the public intimacy and quiet joy at seeing his family reunited.

After a moment, Louis bent down and kissed his son atop the head before pulling him into an embrace.

"You've grown bigger!" Louis exclaimed in English, his French accent pronounced.

Clauvère returned the embrace and protested with a grin. "I haven't grown that much, Père. It's only been two months at most."

Louis laughed warmly, his joy evident.

As Louis, Minuette, and Clauvère gathered near the waiting carriage, the lively crowd fell briefly into silence. Thibault, dressed in his La Pointierre tabard, stood at the open door. The sight of a horse-drawn carriage with the distinguished crest of French nobility was uncommon in Savannah, a city where European titles carried little practical meaning.

Louis turned his attention away from the murmuring crowd and back to his family. "Viens, viens. Allons-y," (Come, come. Let's go.) he said, spreading his arms wide.

As Clauvère, Minuette, and Louis approached the door, whispers moved through the onlookers. Some exchanged curious glances, their brows knit with confusion and intrigue. A few dared voice their astonishment.

"Would you look at that, Martha? French nobility in these parts? And those are well-dressed... negros getting in the carriage with him," an elderly woman murmured to her companion, her voice tinged with disbelief.

The one called Martha leaned closer. "You don't think he's one of those wealthy plantation men, do you? It's a strange sight, to be sure."

Louis glanced toward the onlookers with a composed smile, acknowledging their curiosity without taking offense. He understood that his family presented an unusual sight in this new world, where free persons of mixed heritage were rarely seen in such company.

Minuette leaned closer to her son. "Ma chérie, que disent-ils?" (My dearest, what are they saying?) Minuette inquired, her voice laced with curiosity.

Clauvère furrowed his brow, clearly reluctant to repeat the words. After a quiet sigh, he translated the remarks for his mother as gently as he could, assuring her that the townsfolk had likely never encountered mulattos before.

Seeing the unease this caused her son, Minuette drew him close, resting a comforting arm around his shoulder. She reassured him in her soothing voice, "Tout va bien, ma chérie. Ils ne savent pas que leurs paroles peuvent blesser." (It's alright, my dearest. They don't know that their words can wound.)

Clauvère nodded, and smiling faintly said, "Oui, maman." (Yes, mother.)

Minuette guided him to the steps of the carriage. As they climbed inside, the murmurs of the crowd followed them for a moment longer before the spectators gradually dispersed.

Soon the carriage rolled away, carrying the de La Pointierre family toward their new home.

The carriage came to a halt before a stately white house, its wraparound porch nestled amidst moss-draped oaks. Night had fully descended, veiling the house's exterior in darkness. Clauvère strained his eyes to take in its grandeur, though with little success, before following his father inside.

Footfalls behind him drew his attention. A brief glance over his shoulder revealed the coachman carrying their luggage into the house. Their trunks had been collected earlier and brought separately in another carriage.

Candlelight provided the only illumination in the grand foyer, its flickering glow dancing across the polished hardwood floors. It was clear that Louis could scarcely contain his excitement at unveiling their new home to his wife and their son.

Guided by his father, Clauvère and his mother began a tour of the house. Each room opened before them for inspection, revealing decorations that were tasteful and understated. The approving smile upon Minuette's face was soon mirrored by her son, whose sense of wonder was impossible to conceal.

"Father, this place is grander than anything I could have imagined!" Clauvère exclaimed, his eyes wide.

Louis tousled his son's hair, pride warming his expression. "It's our home now, and we'll make it even grander."

He then turned to Minuette. "Actually, now that you are here, mon trésor, there is no need to make it grander."

Minuette performed a graceful curtsy. "Merci beaucoup, mon ami." (Thank you very much, my love.)

Eventually, Louis led his son to his room. After a goodnight hug and a kiss from his mother and father, Clauvère settled into his new surroundings. He prepared himself for bed, after retrieving his night garments from his trunk. The excitement of the day quickly carried him into a deep and peaceful slumber.

MINUETTE NOTETTE
de LA POINTIERRE

2

As the de La Pointierre family settled into their new home, their lives began to intertwine with the rhythms of the bustling city. Louis had secured a place that represented their dreams of a bright future, and Clauvère was soon to take his first steps into a new school.

Clauvère greeted the grand foyer early in the morning, much like the sunlight that streamed through the tall windows. He carried with him an eager heart ready to embrace a new day.

"Clauvère," Louis called out, a warm smile accompanying the announcement as he found his son exploring the new home. "I have some news for you. I've already scouted out a fine school for you to attend. How do you feel about starting?"

Clauvère's face lit up with enthusiasm, his readiness evident in his bright smile. He possessed a sharp mind and a strong desire to test his knowledge against the children of the American colonies, eager to see where he stood among them.

Louis, a man of ambition, had high hopes for his son, Clauvère. He wanted to ensure that Clauvère learned the ways of colonial America and received a proper colonial education. To achieve this, he had made arrangements to enroll his son in a local school before the teachers discovered his mixed racial heritage.

On that sunny morning, Louis accompanied Clauvère to the grand entrance of the colonial school. The headmaster's raised eyebrow was the first sign that their plan might encounter obstacles.

"What can I do for you, Count de La Pointierre?" the headmaster asked, a hint of skepticism in his tone.

Louis chose not to correct the man regarding his proper noble title, deeming it a matter of little consequence in the American colonies where the significance of nobility carried less weight.

"We spoke a while back about my son, Clauvère. I wish to enroll him in your school today," Louis replied. His voice brimmed with determination as he presented a wax-sealed envelope from an inner pocket of his jacket. "Here is a letter of introduction from Mr. Hartford."

The headmaster remained aloof, refusing to acknowledge the proffered correspondence, let alone spare a moment to examine its contents. "Is this your son, Count de La Pointierre?" he inquired.

Louis turned his gaze down to Clauvère, his chest swelling with paternal pride, and with a broad smile, he placed his hand firmly on his son's shoulder. "Yes, indeed. This is my son."

Clauvère sensed a disquieting undertone in the headmaster's demeanor. He couldn't quite place the cause but he felt it none-the-less. He darted a quick glance from the headmaster to his father, silently assessing whether Louis shared his unease. Judging by his father's expression, Clauvère suspected that his father Louis was either blissfully unaware of the underlying tension or adeptly concealing his awareness. It happened to be the former.

The headmaster leaned in, speaking in a hushed tone. "I'm sorry, Count de La Pointierre, but if he is your son, he cannot attend this school."

"Why is that?" Louis inquired with a gentle tone.

The headmaster's demeanor faltered, evident in the disdainful curl of his nose. "When you first spoke with me about enrolling your son in our school, you did not mention his..." he looked at Clauvère down the bridge of his nose. "...condition," he finally finished.

The headmaster looked back at Louis. "Negros do not attend here. And they do not learn here, Count de La Pointierre." The headmaster spoke as if this were common knowledge.

Without uttering another word, Louis turned away. Clauvère, well-acquainted with his father's expressions, could discern the immense effort Louis was exerting to restrain his anger. Disheartened but not defeated, Louis left the school with Clauvère by his side. He decided that he was going to seek an alternative solution.

In that bewildering moment, Clauvère felt an unsettling mix of emotions coursing through him. Having grown up in the vibrant heart of Martinique, where he and his family were embraced by a warm and diverse community, he had never experienced the cruel sting of racism firsthand.

This was especially true since he was the son of nobility. It was as though the world had suddenly shifted, and he was adrift in unfamiliar waters. Clauvère couldn't comprehend why anyone would judge him based on the hue of his skin, a criterion so foreign to him. His father, standing firm and unyielding against the headmaster's prejudice, filled him with an immense sense of pride.

Clauvère's father had attempted to get Clauvère accepted at the local school, a place that held both the promise of knowledge and the sting of discrimination. Upon rejection, he chose not to raise his voice in argument. He just left with his son.

Louis glanced down at his son as they walked away from the school. The boy, once so eager to face the world, now studied the cobblestones beneath his feet with unusual quiet. It struck Louis that this was the first time he had seen his son hesitate so. Become so withdrawn.

Later, back in his study, Louis shared his frustration with George Hartford, his business partner. George was sympathetic and suggested an alternative: hiring a tutor for Clauvère.

Louis sighed, his face reflecting the hurdles he'd already faced. "I've considered that, George, but no tutor I've approached is willing to teach him. I tried most of the afternoon, sending out letters of inquiry. It seems the headmaster spoke of this with others."

"That is distressing. I cannot understand why individuals would cling to the notion that the color of one's skin can easily determine the intelligence of the individual," George said.

Louis held a brandy sniffer in his hand, its contents swirling within, as he pondered why he had allowed himself to drink so early in the evening. After a moment's reflection, he realized that it was his anger driving his decisions, not his own will. Setting the brandy sniffer down, he turned to George.

"These Englishmen are ignorant, George. You won't find this treatment occurring in France. They are civilized there," Louis uttered with pride.

George took that slight in hand and dismissed it from his mind. He knew that Louis meant no harm in the statement. He leaned back, his mind at work. "Well, I might have a remedy for you, my friend. How about my eldest daughter, Amelia, tutoring Clauvère?"

Louis seemed to brighten perceptively at the idea. He was not only enthusiastic about solving the issue of his son's education but also about the potential for their families to grow closer. George's suggestion of his own daughter serving as a tutor for Louis's son held the promise of strengthening their familial bonds and deepening the trust in their business relationship.

"I believe that's a wonderful idea, George. When can we start?" Louis asked eagerly, his excitement apparent.

Clauvère had been sitting quietly in the parlor busy with a book in his lap. Upon hearing this, he couldn't help but smile, observing his father's enthusiasm. It was evident that Louis was even more excited about him starting school than he was, evidence of his father's desire to provide Clauvère a good education.

George, in response to his business partner's enthusiasm, smiled back. He was pleased that such a simple solution could resolve the educational issue. George recognized the importance of maintaining a positive relationship with a Frenchman from the West Indies, especially one with the title of Count. The potential benefits of their continued collaboration were substantial, and he genuinely liked Louis as a person.

"I believe I can provide you with an answer before the end of the day. Let me return home and discuss this with my daughter," George offered as a way to expedite the process.

Louis interrupted George before he could leave. "Hold on. I can't have you doing something for me without compensation." Louis's hand cupped his chin, and his eyes focused on the floor before him. "I propose paying your daughter two pounds sterling a month," Louis stated as his hand made a sudden, affirmative gesture.

George was taken aback by the generosity of the offer. Although he was initially inclined to accept such a significant amount, he considered that this was something that Louis should negotiate directly with his daughter. After all, it was her services that he was seeking. George recognized the importance of encouraging his daughters to be self-sufficient and not solely reliant on a man for their livelihood.

Despite Amelia only being fifteen, he was confident that she would be able to handle her own financial affairs as far as this was concerned.

"How about you discuss the salary with Amelia, Louis," George suggested, emphasizing the importance of his daughter's agency. "I'll send her your way later this evening to work out the details."

Louis expressed his gratitude with a warm smile and stepped closer to George, patting him on the back in thanks. He then guided George towards the front door of the house.

George returned to the de La Pointierre residence a few hours later, his daughter, Amelia, standing quietly beside him. Louis, Minuette, and Clauvère received them at the door, and Louis ushered them inside with practiced cordiality.

"George, you've yet to meet the family," Louis announced, resting a proud hand on his son's shoulder. "This is Clauvère."

He turned then, and a smile — one rare even to himself — touched his features. "And this is my wife, Minuette."

Minuette stepped forward, a gloved hand extended with quiet grace.

"Enchantée de faire votre connaissance. Mon mari m'a souvent parlé de vous avec les plus grands éloges," (Pleased to make your acquaintance. My husband has often spoken of you with the highest praise.) she said, her voice clear and measured, carrying the delicate timbre of crystal struck by wind.

George found himself caught in her gaze. For an instant, his composure slipped — the polite phrase forming on his tongue faltered before he recovered it with a shallow bow.

"Nice to meet you," he murmured, uncertain of her words but certain of their gentleness. He glanced toward Louis for confirmation; a brief translation followed before he turned back to her.

"I'm glad," he added, his voice lower. "I hope we get along."

She inclined her head in acknowledgment, a faint smile softening her expression. The simple motion seemed to still the air between them. Then, as if suddenly aware of his own hesitation, George cleared his throat and looked aside, turning his attention toward the introductions that awaited him. Her silence, unforced and serene, made it easier.

"Louis, this is my daughter, Amelia," he said at last.

Clauvère studied the beautiful, brunette woman—no, teen girl, who would be his tutor. She was nearly a foot taller than him, but still shorter than both her father and his own. Her slim figure and warm smile made a favorable impression. Clauvère's attention returned to George, who continued speaking.

"I forgot to tell you that the deal includes an addition," George added with a hint of mischief.

"What do you mean?" Louis inquired.

George looked down and behind himself. Emerging from behind his legs was a petite little girl with striking platinum blonde hair that more closely resembled white than anything else.

"This is my other daughter, the youngest, Penelope. She's twelve years old like your son. Her sister tutors her as well. I don't believe you've ever met her," George offered. "She rarely gets out of the house," he confessed as well.

Louis laughed lightly. "Delighted," he offered in greeting to the girls.

Penelope appeared like a small, timid creature, clinging to her father's pant leg and only cautiously peeking from behind his protective frame.

Minuette's eyes softened at the sight. She stepped forward and lowered herself to the little girls eye level. "Elle est charmante et adorable. Comme une petite poupée," (She's enchanting and adorable. Like a little doll.) she murmured with a tender smile.

Louis provided a quick translation for George and Amelia, his voice carrying a note of fond amusement. Both laughed softly in response, the tension of formality easing just a little.

Clauvère, emboldened by the gentle atmosphere, blurted out softly under his breath, "She doesn't look anything like you," without considering his words. He had not meant to be heard but he had been nonetheless.

Minuette turned. "Clauvère," she called out in dismay.

Louis moved to reprimand his son, but George intervened. He squatted down to be at eye level with Clauvère, resting his hands on his knees and engaging the boy with a smile.

"You're right," George admitted. He looked up at Amelia. "Of the two of them, my oldest resembles me the most."

George partially turned and motioned for Penelope to come closer. She took two steps and nestled herself under his arm, seeking solace.

George turned back to Clauvère and said with pride, "This little angel looks exactly like her late mother. She's shy, so you have to be gentle with her."

"Say hello to Clauvère, Penelope," George encouraged.

Penelope cast Clauvère a stern look, then clutched her father's jacket in her small fists, burying her face in the side of his chest.

For some inexplicable reason, Clauvère's heart quickened, and a warm flush colored his cheeks when Penelope fixed him with that intense gaze. He speculated that she was likely of the same date of birth, perhaps only a month or two older or younger.

George chuckled, straightening up while scooping Penelope into his arms. He turned to Louis and Minuette. "You have to forgive her. She doesn't speak. Doctors say she isn't simple. She just stopped speaking when her mother passed away."

Louis nodded in understanding, then turned to translate what had been said to Minuette, who had likely caught only the fringes of its meaning. When he finished, she smiled at the child and reached out her arms. To her surprise, Penelope opened hers at once and allowed herself to be gathered close.

Sunlight poured through the tall windows, softening the air around them as Minuette held the girl against her. George and Amelia watched with mingled confusion and wonder. Clauvère looked on in a brief flicker of jealousy before accepting that his mother's embrace was no longer his alone.

Louis smiled quietly, sensing that his partner's family and his own had drawn closer in so short a time.

George, still watching his daughter nestled against Minuette's shoulder, scratched his head in quiet bewilderment. "Well, I'll be," he murmured—half to himself, as if unsure he'd truly seen what he had.

The next morning's light was bright as Louis sat in his study. He passed pages of documents from one side of his desk, scanned them quickly and efficiently and passed them to the other side. All the while he worried that the headmaster's cruelty from the day before might dull his son's spirit.

He had time to pursue this thought as a single carriage arrived at the de La Pointierre residence, bearing the young woman from the previous day with a pile of books and an air of determination. Amelia Hartford, followed along by Penelope, had come to assist Clauvère in his studies.

The hallway outside Louis's study was quiet enough that Amelia could hear the faint scratch of a quill moving within. She hesitated, fingers brushing the folds of her skirt, the polished wood of the door reflecting her own uneasy face.

Her father's words echoed—You'll speak with the Chevalier yourself, my dear. It's your arrangement now.

It had felt, at the time, like trust. Now it felt suspiciously like abandonment.

She drew a breath and rapped her knuckles gently against the door. The sound seemed to carry too far down the corridor.

"Yes?" came Louis's voice from within, clipped but not unkind.

"It's Amelia Hartford, My Lord," she said quickly, then caught herself. "May I come in?"

"Of course. Entrez, mademoiselle."

She opened the door to find him behind a heavy desk, surrounded by neat stacks of parchment and the scent of ink and sealing wax. Sunlight cut across the room, touching the polished brass buckles of his coat. He did not rise immediately—his eyes moved across a document until, noticing her curtsy, he set the paper aside and smiled faintly.

"There's no need for that," he said, gesturing lightly with one hand. "We're not at court, and you've no cause to tremble before me. Sit, if you please."

His tone was kind, the sort of gentleness that only deepened her nervousness. She crossed the room and perched on the edge of the chair opposite his desk, hands folded tightly in her lap.

"I understand you've come to discuss your terms," Louis began, his accent smoothing the edges of his English. "Your father tells me you are quite capable. Before we speak of remuneration, I wish to be clear about my expectations."

"Yes, My Lord," she answered softly.

He paused mid-sentence and glanced up at her, one brow lifting with mild amusement. He said nothing, merely returned his gaze to the page before him, and continued.

"I expect my son's instruction to maintain the discipline he was accustomed to in Martinique. I do not wish him indulged or excused for his temperament—only understood. He learns best when he believes he has earned approval rather than been given it."

"Yes, My Lord," Amelia murmured again, sitting a bit straighter.

Another pause. He looked across his desk, noticing how her hands clutched at her dress as it flowed down her lap. The faintest flicker of a smile touched his mouth, as his eyes returned to the document in his hand. He set it aside and steadied his gaze on her. His elbows greeted the surface of his desk, his chin resting on his hands.

"Above all," he continued, "his lessons must cultivate grace, not pride. Intelligence he already has in abundance."

"Yes, Count. I will—" She froze, realizing her mistake.

He tilted his head, amused. "My father is the Count, mademoiselle. I am a Chevalier."

Color rose to her cheeks as her eyes fell to her lap. "Forgive me—yes, Count—Chevalier de La Pointierre."

He lifted a hand, laughter suppressed but evident in his eyes. "If you insist on formality, Monsieur de La Pointierre will suffice. But I'd rather you spoke as you would to any other man without worry of title. Please, continue."

Amelia inclined her head, a small, embarrassed smile tugging at her lips. The correction had not stung; if anything, it had eased the propriety she'd wrapped around herself.

Amelia inclined her head, embarrassed yet oddly relieved. The stiffness in her shoulders eased. "I only meant that I understand your wishes, Monsieur de La Pointierre," she said carefully. "I'll do my best to meet them."

"Then, please continue with what you were saying."

"Yes, Monsieur de La Pointierre," she said, the name careful on her tongue. "I've taught my sister for some time now. Penelope is a patient pupil, but she knows my ways. I confess I don't yet know how your son learns—or what he'll expect from me."

Louis leaned back slightly, hands steepled still, regarding her with quiet interest. "That, Mademoiselle Hartford, is something you'll discover for yourself. I suspect he will do the same."

He watched as something seemed to ease within her. A shift in thoughts perhaps but definitely a more relaxed feeling as if she'd grown just a bit more comfortable in his presence. He inwardly smiled, appreciating the courage she unconsciously displayed in this gesture. A feeling that she had become, at the least, a little less nervous about speaking with him.

"Yes, Monsieur de La Pointierre," she said quickly.

"Now, let's discuss remuneration."

Louis paused, giving her space to respond, instead he was presented with her seemingly withdrawing within herself again. He assumed it was the case was due to her being responsible for negotiating the terms of her own worth instead of her father doing it for her.

"Is two pounds sterling a month sufficient for your services."

Amelia's mouth opened and closed. She'd already had a hard time believing that she would get paid that amount when her father had told her the day prior. To hear it again, and from her potential employer, gave her pause. That amount was, without question, more generous than necessary and caused her to worry.

'*Father said he trusts me to handle such things. But I wonder if that's trust or convenience. Trust was the word men used when they had decided a thing was no longer a concern*,' she thought. Her father's confidence warmed and unsettled her.

She took a deep breath and looked up from the wreckage her hands had wrought on her dress, ignoring the wrinkles now present in the fine linen.

"Two pounds is generous, sir. But I'd rather you decide it after a week, when you've seen if I'm worth it."

Louis smiled and stood. He rounded the big desk and presented his hand to Amelia who looked up in hesitation before extending her hand into his.

"Then it's decided. Two pounds it is." He gave a soft pull to give her an indication that the conversation had reached conclusion and that she should stand.

Her eyes, soft and uncertain, lifted to his as she rose—unaware that in his warmth he had already decided her worth for her, undoing the humility she had meant as restraint.

Two pounds sterling a month was a rather substantial amount—nearly twice what a governess or educated female tutor could expect. And Amelia was not even an established governess; she was a 15-year-old colonial girl just beginning. Only three years older than the boy she had been commissioned to educate.

Louis' smile disarmed her like nothing else could have. The warmth of his hand was a kindness she had not expected and it lifted her spirit as it eased her worry. The slight bow he gave made her smile in return and, without thinking, she lifted the hem of her dress slightly and curtsied.

Louis led her out of the study and closed the door softly behind her. She stood there, in the hallway, staring at the tops of her shoes, hands clutched in the folds of her dress, as her chest rose and fell rhythmically before slowing down. She heard the sound of a breath being released that she had not known had been held and looked up with confidence. Her gaze turning to the large window and the sunlight spilling in.

Confidence had blossomed because negotiation had been simpler than she feared. Her smile slipped just a small portion but did not fade—the teaching, she suspected, would not be.

She's been teaching Penelope—someone whose affection, grief, and silence she understands.Penelope's silences were soft, familiar things—grief worn smooth by time. But this boy she had yet to meet was of another world entirely. His silence, if he had one, would not yield so easily.

Teaching Penelope was simple. Teaching Clauvère would be performance, scrutiny, risk. She wasn't sure which frightened her more—failing the boy or proving she could succeed.

Other thoughts came to mind. *'He'd opened the door himself—an unnecessary courtesy, yet one she'd remember. Father had always done the same. Perhaps the world wasn't built on station alone—perhaps some walls simply waited for the right hand to open them.'*

Clauvère was next to visit Louis in his office. Upon his son's entrance, he saw only a thoughtful calm in Clauvère's eyes—a kind of quiet puzzlement rather than pain from the experience in rejection of his enrollment in the local school house. It was a clear sign to Louis that his son might not have been as troubled by this new change as he had expected but instead had internalized something else that troubled him. However, he was not fully convinced yet.

Despite that, he chose not to address the issue, giving his son space with which to process the event on his own terms. He was confident that Clauvère would seek his counsel if he needed it. Therefore, instead, he explained to Clauvère his expectations and sent him off to the library where the instruction was to occur.

Amelia and Penelope, a bit apprehensive, sat together in the library awaiting the third to join their party. Clauvère entered, scanned the room and noted the two girl's position. He approached Amelia and stood before her.

With one hand positioned behind his back, his other took hers without preamble. He bent low at the waist, given her seated position, and kissed her hand. “Mademoiselle, I thank you for your kindness in teaching me. I look forward to learning much from you.”

Amelia glanced first at Clauvère, her cheeks flushing hotly, before turning her gaze to her sister. Penelope seemed awestruck. What Amelia knew of her sister’s refusal to communicate instead became a response of astonishment she read from her expression and her eyes.

Amelia turned to Clauvère and stammered, “Um… Well, I think we should get started, My Lord—”

Clauvère cut her off. “Address me simply by name, mademoiselle.”

Her face went hotter. She pulled her hand back gently, rose too quickly, and turned away under the pretense of gathering her materials. The embarrassment clung to her like static. *‘He is younger,’* she scolded herself. *‘And yet he behaves like a man who has spent his life in salons and courts.’*

She moved to the small table Louis had cleared for her, rifling through the stack of books she herself had arranged only that morning. The titles swam uselessly before her eyes—Latin primers, geography texts, arithmetic ledgers—none of which she could seem to think about clearly.

At last she selected a single leather-bound volume, holding it to her chest as though it anchored her. She turned back toward the children.

“Well,” she began, steadying her voice, “before we begin lessons proper, I must know where you stand in your studies.”

Clauvère straightened at once, eager, polite. Penelope shifted in her seat, watching him with that constant quiet alertness Amelia knew so well.

“Let’s start with arithmetic,” Amelia said, opening the book to a simple exercise. “If you have twenty-four francs and spend one-third—”

“Twelve,” Clauvère said too quickly.

Her brows lifted. “Try again.”

Penelope’s small hand lifted as though of its own accord before Clauvère could respond. She touched the tabletop once—deliberate—and then held up three fingers.

Amelia blinked. “Yes, Penny. You’re right. Eight.”

Clauvère looked between them, startled. Color spread across his cheeks.

‘A language I don’t understand?’ he thought.

Penelope dropped her gaze at once, but the faintest smile tugged at her lips. She hadn't spoken—but she had answered.

Amelia cleared her throat gently. "Very good. Let's try another."

For the next several minutes, she asked questions in geography, letters, and sums. A pattern emerged: Clauvère was intelligent—quick, curious, confident—but Penelope matched him in nearly every subject and surpassed him in a handful.

Clauvère masked his surprise poorly. Penelope pretended not to notice, though her small shoulders drew in shy pride each time she answered correctly.

Amelia closed the book slowly.

"Well," she said, more to herself than to them, "I see what I'm working with."

She seated herself at the teaching desk, folding her hands to still their faint trembling. "You're both bright," she continued, meeting each pair of eyes with a firmer confidence than before. "Which means you will learn quickly. And I will expect much from both of you."

Penelope's chin lifted a fraction.

Clauvère nodded, pride straightening his spine.

Amelia felt the first true stirrings of her role settle into place—not the nervous girl in Louis's study, but a young woman beginning to understand responsibility and the quiet authority she could claim.

"Let us begin," she said.

The lesson unfolded gently—ink scratching, pages turning, sunlight warming the wood-paneled room. Penelope's silence was no longer a wall; it was a language of its own. Clauvère's determination, once raw, grew focused under Amelia's direction.

And Amelia, watching them both, realized with a small tightening in her chest that teaching them was not a simple task.

It was two worlds meeting on a tabletop.

When the hour ended, Penelope slipped away first—gliding toward the hall that led to where Minuette sat in the parlor. Clauvère watched her go with a mixture of confusion and something he could not yet name, wondering where she was going off to and not knowing.

Amelia gathered her books, pausing when she caught Clauvère's thoughtful gaze.

"You did well today," she told him.

He nodded, though his expression remained clouded. "She is very clever."

"Yes," Amelia said softly. "She is."

But she said nothing of the other truth—that teaching both of them frightened her and thrilled her and made her feel, for the first time in her life, as though she might truly shape something that mattered.

She would learn him. And he, inevitably, would learn her.

During the first break, Clauvère sat still at the desk he had been using all morning. He considered the disappointment of being told he couldn't attend school with white children in the American colonies. To him, it made no sense. Back on Martinique, being part of the nobility, he'd gone to school with French white boys and girls, and there had never been an issue.

He thought it the most senseless thing imaginable—to judge someone on the tone of their skin. Color, in his mind, should not decide one's place. And truthfully, he had always been the brightest student in his class.

Amelia, sharp as she was, judged him wrongly here. She knew what had happened, and assumed that Clauvère must be in some kind of emotional discomfort. That was far from the truth. He became aware of the misunderstanding when she tried to soothe him about the new learning arrangement.

"Don't worry, Clauvère," Amelia told him. "You'll still receive an excellent education under my guidance."

Clauvère felt no anxiety about the schoolhouse incident. In truth, he felt nothing at all about it now—only confusion as to why such senselessness existed. His discomfort came from something else entirely: Penelope was outperforming him in every subject, and it embarrassed him.

There was also the matter of her seeing everything. During each change of subject, her eyes would drift toward him, assessing, observing, reading him in a way other children never had. Clauvère decided that if he wanted to keep his sanity, he should ignore her and work harder.

After lessons he left the library and went to find his maman. He found her in the parlor. The corners of his mouth dipped before he caught himself—they lifted again into a polite line. Penelope was seated in his maman's lap. He took a seat opposite them, ignoring the small flicker of jealousy that rose, unwanted and immediate.

Penelope kept sneaking glances at him as his maman spoke to her in French and occasionally in broken English, explaining whatever she could as best she could.

A week passed in this manner. Clauvère—friendly by nature—tried his best to make Penelope feel comfortable. He went out of his way to greet her every day, partly out of courtesy, partly out of curiosity about the quiet little girl who spent most hours of the day in his company.

"Hello, Penelope. It's nice to see you today," he greeted her with a warm smile each morning.

Penelope was always taken aback by his kindness, her mouth opening only to close again without sound.

Amelia worked diligently during that time. The two children sat at a polished wooden table in the sunlit library, a map of the world hanging on one wall. Amelia's voice was a soothing balm; her approach to education a revelation. She encouraged questions, curiosity, and thought beyond the narrow confines of any schoolroom.

During these days, Penelope slowly began to open up—but only with Minuette, and only in French. And if anyone else was in the room, she fell silent again. Clauvère noticed it by accident—he would hear her speaking haltingly with his maman, only for her to stop mid-sentence the moment he stepped inside.

As the days passed, their shared education became a constant in the lives of both Penelope and Clauvère. Through knowledge and companionship, they pushed quietly against the boundaries of their world.

Louis noticed the change in his son's demeanor. Amelia had quickly developed a reputation, at least in his eyes, not only for her brilliance but also for her openness. He had worried she might be too cautious or restrained while teaching Clauvère for any number of reasons. That concern proved needless.

One evening, as the sun set behind the live oaks, Louis stood at the entrance of the library watching his son and Penelope bent over their books.

His heart swelled with gratitude for the opportunities this new home had provided. And he knew—with Amelia's help—Clauvère would manage any obstacle life saw fit to place in his path.

Days passed and those days, spent in learning, left little time for Clauvère to explore the grounds of his home. On this particular day, Amelia let Clauvère and Penelope out early, allowing them time to wander around the grounds of the home.

Clauvère was surprised that Penelope had chosen to follow behind him instead of seeking out his mother to spend time with her. It was usually her habit to do so when she was at his home, taking a break from class. Clauvère didn't mind her tagging along at all, in fact, he found it rather comforting to be in her presence.

She chose to walk beside him as he strolled through the tall grass of the field. Penelope's heart swelled with a mixture of emotions. She looked at Clauvère, his light bronze skin illuminated by the fading sun.

She had to admit that he intrigued her. He was unlike any other person that she had met yet. It was mostly due to the fact that she had no exposure to mulattos. Clauvère was also interesting to her in the fact that he did not act as negroes she had heard about from others. She found herself uncertain of what to make of him—only that he intrigued her.

The gentle, late summer breeze whispered through the knee-high grass, causing a gentle sigh to be heard. Clauvère looked to the deep green leaves in the nearby magnolias and smiled. The weather here in Savannah could not have been more different than that of Martinique.

In Savannah, the late summer sun hung high in the sky, casting a relentless and unforgiving heat upon the city. The air was thick and heavy, saturated with humidity that wrapped around you like a stifling blanket.

Clauvère loosed the kerchief wrapped snugly round his neck—an effort to allow air to flow and ease the damp that he felt coming. He had noticed that the people of Savannah sought refuge in the shade of magnolia trees or under the protective awnings of charming shops that lined the streets. Here, he was tempted to do the same for a moment.

Clauvère couldn't help but contrast this warm Savannah evening with the late summers of his childhood. There, the Caribbean breeze would dance through the swaying palm trees, offering a refreshing respite from the sun's warmth. The air was filled with the scent of saltwater and the soothing melody of the ocean waves caressing the shore. The vibrant colors of tropical flowers painted the landscape, and the azure sea stretched to the horizon, inviting anyone to take a refreshing dip.

He found himself yearning for the familiar comfort of Martinique's late summer, where the weather embraced you like a gentle friend rather than a relentless foe. The climate here was quite the contrast, demanding strength and perseverance.

As he looked out at the magnolias before him, he smiled. He couldn't help it. He thought about the unique beauty and challenges of both places. Savannah's sweltering late summer was a stark reminder of the difference between Martinique's lazy breezy days.

Clauvère looked towards Penelope and gave her a gentle smile. He turned from the field and walked back towards the house, ensuring that she followed him and keeping his pace slower, to match hers.

They reached the grand porch and chose to sit on the swinging bench, overlooking the garden before them.

The sun bathed the garden in a warm, golden light as they sat together on the ornate wrought-iron and wooden bench. In silence, they gazed at the majestic trees that stood like ancient sentinels, their lush leaves casting dappled shadows on the ground.

Clauvère's voice was tinged with nostalgia as he spoke, his words a gentle breeze in the stillness. "Penelope, you know, in Martinique, the summers are quite different. The air is warm, but it's a gentle warmth that embraces you, not this relentless heat."

He didn't take his eyes off the magnificent grove of trees before them, as if their grandeur provided a comforting backdrop to the memories he was sharing. "The island is filled with vibrant colors, the scent of tropical flowers, and the sound of the ocean waves that soothe you to sleep every night."

Penelope, her eyes fixed on Clauvère, absorbed every word he spoke, her silent presence in harmony with her willingness to connect with him despite her selective mutism. There was a certain depth in her gaze that conveyed understanding and empathy, as if she, too, longed for the memories of a distant place. Or maybe it was a distant person. Someone not there anymore.

Clauvère's smile was bittersweet, and his fingers absently traced a delicate pattern on the bench's surface. "I used to watch the sunsets over the Caribbean Sea, and they were the most magnificent shades of orange, pink, and purple. Those summer evenings in Martinique, Penelope, they were unforgettable."

Penelope looked down between them, noting that his hand was mere inches from her own. She was tempted to touch his finger tips but kept her impulse in check. She turned to regard Clauvère once more when she noted movement.

He looked over at her, his voice softer, almost intimate. "I've missed those cool summer breezes and the way the warm sand felt beneath my feet as I strolled along the beach."

Penelope remained silent, her eyes locked onto his, sharing in the memories he painted with his words. She felt herself even more strongly drawn to him. As the quiet afternoon continued, it was as though their connection grew stronger through the silence that followed, transcending the need for spoken language. Clauvère, speaking of the summers in Martinique, had found a way to bridge the gap between them, forging a bond with his mere words. No, it was more the cadence of his voice as he had spoken that had done so.

Clauvère's voice.

His voice was soft as the whispers stirring the magnolia leaves above them.

He stood slowly. Eventually, he broke the quietude. The curiosity that had been simmering within him found its way to the surface, and he gently broached a question he had been pondering. This moment, beneath the shade of the garden's ancient trees, felt like the right time to delve into the enigma of Penelope's silence.

"Penelope, I've often wondered, why don't you speak?" Clauvère's words were careful, chosen with a tenderness that mirrored his curiosity.

In response to his inquiry, Penelope turned her gaze away from the warmth of his inquisitive eyes, eyes that had the uncanny ability to draw her in. She focused her attention on her folded hands, which lay still on her lap, and remained in this contemplative stance for a few fleeting moments. Then, with a sense of resolve, she retrieved a small piece of paper and a pencil from her pocket, as though this act alone was significant. With deliberate movements, she began to write her response.

The note that Penelope handed to Clauvère was a window into the thoughts and emotions she had guarded so closely. Her delicate script revealed the vulnerability that had led to her silence. Her words conveyed a story untold, a silent history written on this small piece of paper.

The message was clear, yet fraught with pain. It stated that her words had inflicted wounds before, that they had been the source of hurt and harm. She had seen the consequences of her own voice, a power she had wielded unwittingly, and it had left scars in its wake. Penelope's silence was not a barrier, but a shield to protect against the possibility of causing pain to others, an act of selflessness born from a painful past.

Clauvère read her words, his heart heavy with understanding for the person who had chosen to bear the silence to spare others from suffering.

He lapsed into thoughtful silence for a moment. He took a seat beside her again.

The message Penelope had entrusted to him resonated deeply, touching a chord he hadn't been aware of. It stirred a desire to assist her, to find a way to ease her burden, but he was unsure of where to begin. As he contemplated, a memory emerged from the recesses of his mind, a fragment of time when he had unknowingly observed Penelope repeating French words spoken by his mother, Minuette, to her.

With a gentle tone, Clauvère ventured to ask, his voice soft as the secrets shared between the flowers and the bees hovering near them. Just there, beneath the ancient magnolia trees. "I hope I'm not prying, but I've noticed you repeating some of the French words my mother has been teaching you. Do you find it different to speak in French than in English?"

Penelope, deep in contemplation, held her thoughts for just long enough to make Clauvère question whether he had crossed a boundary. Eventually, she retrieved the piece of paper and pencil once more, her script meticulous as she penned her response. The message she handed to Clauvère contained another layer of her silent narrative, a glimpse into her hopes and aspirations.

Her words revealed an idea that had taken root in her heart—a belief that speaking in a different language might offer a shield against causing pain. The notion that another language, such as French, might carry her words without her past.

The message haunted Clauvère. It was a complex revelation, laden with the potential for a new beginning, where the power of language could be harnessed to protect and heal, both for herself and others.

Clauvère rose and bowed gently at the waist, his noble bearing evident as he spoke.

A warm smile graced Clauvère's lips as he observed Penelope. In the golden embrace of the setting sun, her platinum blonde hair seemed to come alive, radiating a lustrous glow. He couldn't help but be captivated by her beauty.

"Bonsoir, madame," (Good evening, madam.) he greeted her, his voice carrying the gentle charm of the French language with that unmistakable island charm. "Tu es magnifique sous ce soleil d'après-midi." (You look beautiful in this afternoon sun.)

Penelope's cheeks flushed with a sudden rush of warmth, a brilliant blush that painted her delicate features. Although she hadn't comprehended every word Clauvère had spoken, her grasp of a few French phrases was firm, and the one thing she had unmistakably understood was that he had called her beautiful.

Overwhelmed by both embarrassment and a fluttering heart, she cast her gaze aside. Then, in a moment that held a hint of magic, she broke her silence to Clauvère for the very first time since he had entered her life.

"Merci, monsieur," (Thank you, sir.) she replied, her voice a gentle murmur, soft and melodic.

Penelope, Clauvère, and Amelia
As children together

3

George Hartford and Louis de La Pointierre huddled in earnest discussion in Louis' study. Their shared concern was matters related to the import business.

George's brows knitted with concern as he spoke. "Louis, these taxes are cutting into our profit margin. Our business, so carefully built, isn't as solid as it should be."

Louis nodded, mirroring George's unease. "Indeed, George. The stability we should be enjoying isn't there. We must consider how these changes will affect us in the long run."

As they mulled over their concerns, George's youngest, Penelope, clung to her father's side. Not with touch but distance. Her large, expressive eyes bore a weight of unspoken fears, a mirror to the haunting loss of her mother. She dreaded the thought of losing her father as well, and her attempts to draw his attention were often met with affectionate but gentle rejections. George would often guide her toward her older sister, Amelia, who had assumed the mantle of looking after her in the absence of their mother.

Clauvère, watching from across the room, noticed the change in her. Since that afternoon beneath the magnolias, she had not spoken again. He'd thought the moment had marked a beginning, but it seemed instead to have left her overwhelmed—perhaps frightened by how easily her voice had returned only to vanish again. He wondered if she regretted speaking at all, or if the act had simply stirred feelings she wasn't ready to face.

For Penelope, the memory of that day clung to her quietly like a whisper she could not quite forget. But, it had been so long since she'd spoken aloud that the sound of her own voice had startled her. The warmth of Clauvère's kindness had made it possible in the moment, but afterward she felt exposed, as though she had been pulled into the open. She sought refuge in silence once more, and now, unable to name her unease, she hovered near her father for comfort.

George gave Penelope a gentle, reassuring smile. "Penelope, my dear, why don't you go help your sister for now? We have important matters to discuss."

With a nod, Penelope complied, yet her unspoken longing for her father's company remained palpable. She moved near her sister for a while and eventually found herself in Minuette's arms.

Penelope, with her youthful curiosity, had often found solace in her mother's presence. The memories of her mother's nurturing embrace and soft words still echoed in her mind. Her mother's absence was a constant ache in her heart, and as she watched her father and Louis discussing the import business, she couldn't help but wonder how different things might have been if her mother were still there to provide comfort and guidance.

Even though her father's attention was often consumed by business matters, Penelope had a way of subtly influencing the family dynamics. She had inherited her mother's gentleness and grace, and this often acted as a soothing balm for her sister, Amelia, who had taken on the role of caretaker in their mother's absence. Amelia found solace in Penelope's presence, and it was Penelope's quiet encouragement that had initially prompted her to assume responsibility for her younger sister.

George returned his focus to Louis. "Maybe it's time we consider more than just business. It's been months since your family's arrival. We should get together for dinner tonight. We ought to consider their welfare too."

His gaze drifted toward the women. Minuette was kneeling beside Penelope, her French words lilting and soft as she coaxed a smile from the girl.

Minuette's interactions with Penelope had increased and radiated warmth, care, and understanding, transcending the language barrier that separated them. Penelope, who had adopted selective mutism, and Minuette, who spoke no English, shared an unspoken connection that defied linguistic differences. The bond between them was deepening, and it was increasingly evident that Penelope found comfort in Minuette's company.

A thought occurred to George as he regarded the two. "Amelia has been teaching Penelope and Clauvère; perhaps she can teach Minuette English as well—make her feel more at home here in the colonies."

"She can understand you," Louis said with a faint smile, "though she refuses to use English unless it is absolutely required. Her English isn't..." He shifted in his seat, glanced over at Minuette before turning back to George. "...not perfect. Truth be told, she has never much cared for the language. She insists it sounds rather barbaric beside French."

Louis allowed a small pause after the remark, as though considering whether he had said too much.

Then he added more lightly, "Besides, Clauvère tried to teach her formally but couldn't bring himself to correct his mother. The emotional awkwardness made both uncomfortable."

"Well, perhaps Amelia might still help your wife with her English," George suggested. "Not lessons, precisely—just conversation, you know, being her companion. Since she understands it well enough, speaking it more often might make her feel more at ease here."

Louis chuckled lightly. "A fair thought, my friend. Mon trésor knows the language, but she has never much cared for its sound. She finds it... less musical than our own."

George smiled at that, sensing affection behind his friend's words. "Well, perhaps a companion will persuade her otherwise."

Louis acknowledged George's suggestion with a nod. "That's a great idea, George. One that I am sure that mon trésor (my treasure) would love," Louis responded, calling his wife by her pet name. Louis communicated this to his beloved. She smiled radiantly, pulling Penelope into her arms, giving the unsuspecting girl a small fright to which she gave a whoop.

Everyone laughed. The shared concern for their loved ones continued to deepen the bond between their families.

With the gradual shift from their initial worries to more lighter matters, the two men took their leave of the women and children and proceeded out towards their shared offices in town. The world around them underwent a small transformative renewal with their decision. The Hartford and de La Pointierre families would continue to exchange visits, finding comfort in their growing close-knit companionship.

Later on during that particularly bright day, the three children embarked on a new adventure, beckoned by the vibrant beauty of spring and the welcome of the out of doors. Clauvère took Penelope and Amelia out on a walk towards the boundaries of his family's land. His destination was towards a creek that the house staff had told him of. He desired to see what he could see of the area and learn more about the land on which he now lived.

As the children ventured towards the creek, Penelope's presence became a unifying force. Her mood had softened from her earlier hesitancy. Her ability to find joy in the simplicity of the natural world was infectious.

She was the first to notice the colorful wildflowers that lined the path, and her laughter was like a melody that echoed through the woods, drawing the other two closer to her. Her genuine, unspoken warmth and kindness made her a beloved companion, and even the stoic Clauvère couldn't help but be charmed by her quiet charisma. His earlier concern for her wellbeing seemed to have melted away. Cast aside like a heavy coat in the summer that engulfed them.

The picturesque creek that meandered through the woods was on the border of the property. There were no fences to divide the land or prevent outsiders from wandering through.

Once there, Penelope, Clauvère, and Amelia made a delightful discovery. They stumbled upon Peter Williams, a recent addition to the neighborhood, a white boy who had moved there not long ago.

Peter was wading, barefoot, through a shallow part of the creek. It being a rather warm day, Clauvère could understand his desire to do so. Clauvère decided to be friendly and greet the intruder on his family estate and not make much of it.

He approached the creek, his footsteps un-disturbing of the peaceful atmosphere of the woods. With a friendly smile, he greeted Peter, "Bonjour, I'm Chevalier Clauvère de La Pointierre. I didn't expect to find someone else enjoying this lovely creek."

Peter looked up, a bit startled but not alarmed. He returned the smile, albeit somewhat cautiously. "Hey, I'm Peter. Nice to meet you. I'm new to the area."

Amelia and Penelope joined Clauvère, and Amelia added, "We're just exploring here too. The creek is a wonderful find, don't you think?"

Peter's apprehension seemed to ease as he saw the friendly nature of the newcomers. "Yeah, it sure is. I've only been here a short while, so I'm still discovering all the hidden gems. Are you folks from around here?"

Clauvère chuckled, "No, my family and I just moved here recently. My family's originally from Martinique, but we've come to settle in this beautiful place." He turned to regard the girls, "These two ladies are from Savannah, though."

Peter nodded and offered a warm greeting, "Well, welcome to the neighborhood." Taking a moment to size up Clauvère, he couldn't help but notice the impeccable attire and well-spoken manner. Peter's curiosity got the best of him, and he blurted out towards Amelia and Penelope, "Is he your slave? He's rather well dressed and speaks well."

Amelia's face paled, her gaze shifting apologetically to Clauvère, while Penelope blushed intensely, her cheeks ablaze as though set on fire.

Amelia, eager to clarify, declared with fervor, "He is not a slave! He is the son of a French noble. This land belongs to his family."

Peter was taken aback. He looked at the ground beneath his feet before returning his gaze and regarding the young boy in front of him. He had no inkling that French nobility resided in Savannah, let alone in such close proximity to his own home.

Clauvère, diplomatically choosing to overlook Peter's faux pas, averted his gaze and refrained from making eye contact as Amelia defended him.

Stumbling for the proper address, Peter mumbled, "I'm sorry, My Lord."

Clauvère turned to him with a gentle smile, his voice understanding, "It's okay. This is new to me as well. I've never experienced this kind of behavior due to the color of my skin."

Relieved by Clauvère's response, Peter replied, "Well, I'm glad you accept my apology, My Lord."

Clauvère raised a reassuring hand, saying, "You don't have to call me that. Just call me Clauvère."

The three newcomers and Peter continued to chat by the creek, forging the beginning of a newfound friendship.

Peter found himself utterly entranced by Clauvère's impeccable manners and impressive demeanor. It was the first time he had engaged in conversation with a free negro, and his curiosity shone through vividly. Realizing his initial error, he quickly amended his appellation, recognizing that it was not just any black person he was conversing with but a black *French noble.*

Peter, his eyes wide with wonder, expressed his admiration. "You're incredibly well-mannered. I've never met a negro person like you before."

Clauvère, unfortunately getting accustomed to such responses, greeted Peter's fascination with a warm smile. "Thank you, Peter. We can all learn from each other."

Penelope observed with a smile as the two boys gleefully splashed around in the cool waters a bit later, their laughter echoing through the air. She held a deep appreciation for Clauvère's company, and over time, her heart began to open to Peter as well, despite her enduring silence. The quartet, brought together by the warmth of spring, found joy by the creek's side.

Although often characterized by her quiet nature, Penelope eagerly joined in the boys' explorations along the creek. With each passing minute, Penelope's role in the group evolved. Her gentle nature began to shine, and she wasn't merely an observer; she was an active participant in the discoveries and adventures.

She joined Peter to find the best spots for trying to climb trees and skipping stones along the creek. Her presence added a unique and essential dynamic to the group, and it was clear that her influence extended far beyond her silent observations. Meanwhile, Amelia contentedly watched from the sidelines, amazed to see her sister opening up to yet another person.

In the days that followed, Peter's initial fascination with Clauvère and Penelope blossomed into a genuine friendship. The trio soon became frequent visitors to the nearby creek, and their bond deepened with every outing. Amelia, being a bit older, didn't participate as much but was never fully absent.

In the following weeks, the Hartford and de La Pointierre families had become even more close-knit. Their lives intertwined through business, shared lessons for their children, and frequent dinners that blurred the line between partnership and kinship.

In the cozy parlor of the Hartford family estate, the warm glow of candlelight bathed the room in a soft, inviting radiance. Dinner had just concluded, leaving a tranquil atmosphere that allowed for more intimate interactions. Penelope, her usually bound platinum blond hair cascading gracefully over her shoulders, sat on an ornate couch. It was a rare occasion for her to wear her hair down, a subtle sign of her comfort in the familiar setting. She couldn't help but hope that Clauvère would take notice of this departure from her usual style.

Clauvère, occupying a nearby armchair, exuded an air of quiet dignity through his impeccable posture. He longed to be closer to Penelope but was uncertain if their budding friendship had reached the stage where such proximity would be welcomed. George, Louis, and Minuette, along with Amelia, soon joined them in the parlor. Their faces reflected a mixture of mild concern as the conversation began, each character's dynamics subtly shifting in the gathering's atmosphere.

George had called them over for dinner to allow the families to bond and to discuss his minor trepidation about the growing tensions between the English crown and the American colonies. As they gathered in the cozy sitting room of the Hartford estate, the flickering candles cast dancing shadows on the polished mahogany furniture. Louis, with his well-groomed beard and a thoughtful expression, held a glass of brandy as he discussed the latest developments in the colonies with George, whose face was etched with some concern.

"The rumors are disquieting," Louis remarked, his voice low. "The tension between the colonists and the Crown is reaching a boiling point. It may affect our business significantly."

George nodded, taking a sip from his own glass. "We must prepare for the possibility of a tumultuous future. Our families' livelihoods do depend on our sugar trade."

As the men continued their conversation, Amelia and Minuette sat across from them. Clauvère provided a running translation for his mother's benefit. She was attentive but a bit disengaged from the conversation, her distance stemming more from not yet fully grasping the language than from any lack of interest in what was being communicated. Clauvère kindly gave her the link she needed and she pitched in where she could.

Amelia, dressed in a flowing gown, spoke with a thoughtful tone. "It's disheartening to hear about the violence that's escalating due to the Whigs and Tories. There's talk of seeking independence from the British crown but is that necessary?"

Louis said, "The news from across the sea is troubling as well, with the conclusion of the Seven Years' War just a few years ago things are difficult in Europe. The war had significant financial and military consequences for Great Britain and France. Both King Louis XVI's and King George III's governments are facing significant financial difficulties. The Seven Years' War drained the royal treasury of both kingdoms so it seems they are seeking to refill their coffers through the colonies."

George, dressed in his gentlemanly attire, nodded in agreement. "Unfortunately, this has led to increased taxation and tightened colonial control, causing dissatisfaction," said George.

Minuette, who had been quietly listening, leaned forward slightly, her eyes thoughtful. She spoke softly in French, her words carrying the calm conviction of someone who had never seen such turmoil before and was aptly concerned for those she cared about.

"It trouble is..." began Minuette before she switched languages. "Les rois se disputent, mais ce sont toujours les familles qui paient le prix," (The kings quarrel, but it is always the families who pay the price.)

"Maman says," Clauvère began translating gently as he relayed her words.

A hush followed, her voice lingering in the air like the fading note of a hymn. Even George, who had been ready with a response, merely nodded, his gaze thoughtful.

Amelia chimed in, "The Boston Massacre did little to help matters. Now both the Whigs and Tories oppose one another much more openly."

Clauvère, with a thoughtful expression, looked toward Louis. "Papa, do you think these conflicts will ever come to an end? It's hard to fathom the suffering that's happening in this land and across the sea."

"Mon fils," (my son) Louis began. "There is no telling. The trade disruptions are affecting not only the economy here, but also the lives of those who rely on these goods for their livelihoods, both here and abroad."

Clauvère, his gaze fixed on the floor, whispered to himself in a somber tone, "The troubles of the world can feel overwhelming at times." He was referring to the newfound prejudice he had begun to encounter, a truth that unsettled him more deeply than he cared to admit.

The thought lingered as he lifted his eyes to Penelope. What stirred in him then had no clear shape, no reason he could name—only the feeling that the pressure of the world and the quiet gravity of her presence pressed upon him in the same way. Both were more than he could bear to understand, and beneath it all, he sensed something within him shifting—and that she was somehow part of it.

Mr. Hartford smiled warmly at Clauvère's words, recognizing the wisdom in his young perspective. "Clauvère is right. The world may be filled with challenges, but it is important to believe that through unity and empathy, change can be sparked."

Louis laughed lightly, "But it's important to remember that even in the midst of such turmoil, friendships and connections like ours can bring hope and understanding."

As the conversation flowed, Penelope and Clauvère exchanged knowing glances, a silent affirmation of their own growing bond. In that moment, sitting amidst the flickering candlelight and the echoing voices of their parents discussing weighty matters, Penelope and Clauvère's friendship shone as a beacon of unity and understanding—a small but powerful demonstration of the possibility of harmony amidst the chaos of the outside world.

Penelope, with her vibrant eyes, eventually stared into the distance. She had suffered a tragedy that left her struggling with unspeakable trauma, leaving her silent and distant but she wanted that to change. With Clauvère near her, she felt that she could. Penelope's attention was drawn to her father when he moved.

George leaned back in his chair, rubbing his chin thoughtfully. "Indeed, unity and empathy are crucial. The troubles across the ocean and in America are reminders that we must cherish the peace and build stability where we are in the world. We should work towards a better world for all."

During this time, Minuette had begun spending her afternoons with Amelia, polishing her English through gentle conversation when Amelia was not engaged with teaching. She had always understood the language, but using it aloud still felt foreign on her tongue—its rhythm heavier, less graceful than the French she loved.

Yet Amelia's warmth and curiosity made the practice feel easy. When Minuette faltered, Amelia filled the gaps with laughter and patient encouragement. Their exchanges became less about words and more about companionship—a quiet bridging of two worlds, carried not by grammar but by kindness.

Meanwhile, Penelope remained ensconced in her cocoon of silence, her select mutism still active. It cast a heavy shadow over her as it seemed to leave her isolated outside of the interactions of everyone. The room buzzed with conversation about business, politics, and the uncertain future, but Penelope's isolation was palpable. George often stole glances in her direction, his heart heavy with concern for the daughter he loved.

Penelope's attention was singularly devoted to those fleeting moments when Clauvère stole glances in her direction, though. She was unaware of any other glances thrown her way.

The others in the room, but most notably George, were far from oblivious to this endearing dynamic. Hidden smiles of amusement were discreetly exchanged among them as they collectively observed Clauvère's attempts at surreptitious glances towards Penelope, and her telltale blushes in response.

In this room, they were more than business associates; they were a network of support, a family bonded by shared aspirations and worries. And as the flickering candles bathed the room in their warm, gentle light, each person carried their own burdens and hopes, forging connections and nurturing growth amidst the challenges that lay ahead.

Eventually, Clauvère found himself yearning for a change of scenery. In a soft, heartfelt apology, spoken in his native French to his parents, he politely excused himself from the gathering in the parlor. Penelope, her curiosity piqued, observed his departure with keen interest.

Clauvère had a lot on his mind as he wandered the elegant halls of the Hartford residence. Recent encounters with the harsh realities of the world had left him unsettled, and he felt adrift, questioning his identity as an individual. While he treasured the warm embrace and acceptance of the Hartford family, he knew that such open-mindedness was a rarity in the colonial Americas.

Everywhere he and his mother went, they encountered challenges. Veiled stares, whispered comments, confrontational gazes—all were a daily reminder that he was no longer in Martinique. Clauvère could feel those judgmental eyes bearing down on him.

The contrast with his life in Martinique couldn't be starker. Back there, he was nobility, born to the first son of a Comte, a position that afforded him a unique standing and respect. He had anticipated some difference in treatment upon moving to the American colonies, but the harsh reality he faced was beyond his expectations. It left him grappling with a profound sense of displacement and longing for the comfort and acceptance he had once known.

Thoughts of Penelope were a comforting anchor in the midst of this harsh new reality. Even in so short a time, she was becoming his only source of solace, a steadfast presence in a world that seemed to have turned its back on him.

Clauvère stepped outside and onto the porch. The aroma of freshly cooked cuisine still lingered in the air, mingling with the sweet scent of magnolia blossoms that adorned the estate. It was a tranquil evening, the air alive with the chorus of crickets and the distant hoot of an owl.

Clauvère's eyes, dark and contemplative, lifted to the heavens. The sky above was painted with a tapestry of stars, each one a brilliant beacon in the twilight. It was a sight to behold, a celestial wonder that seemed to bridge the gap between the old world and the new. Clauvère couldn't help but be captivated by the sheer vastness of the universe and the infinite possibilities it held.

As he stood there, the worries of the world seemed to lift from his shoulders. The conversations from the parlor echoed in his mind—the concerns about political unrest, business disruptions, and the uncertain future. But here, under the blanket of the Southern sky, those worries felt distant, like fleeting clouds passing before a boundless horizon.

He walked down the porch steps, his footsteps muffled by the lush grass that stretched out before him. The verdant lawn felt cool and welcoming underfoot. Clauvère wandered further into the garden, the grass brushing against his polished shoes, and the evening breeze tousling his dark, wavy hair.

His thoughts drifted as he walked, unspooling with every slow step. The camaraderie between the two families, the newfound friendship with Penelope, and the challenges they all faced seemed to converge in his mind. The world was changing, that much was certain, but perhaps amidst the turmoil, there was room for more. The bond he was forming with the Hartfords let him cling to that hope.

With each step, the stars above seemed to grow brighter, and Clauvère's heart felt lighter. The vastness of the universe, the countless stars, and the serene beauty of the night sky reminded him of the grandeur of life, the possibilities that existed beyond the confines of their immediate concerns.

Finally, he reached a point where the grass was soft and inviting. He lay down, his eyes fixed on the twinkling above. The whispers of the evening breeze and the gentle rustle of leaves in the trees serenaded him as he gazed upwards. The world felt vast, but for a moment, as he lay on that Southern lawn, he felt a profound connection to the universe, and an overwhelming sense of peace washed over him.

Under the watchful eye of the heavens, Clauvère closed his eyes, his mind filled with the promise of a new day, and the enduring hope that their growing friendships could help navigate the uncertain waters of the changing world.

In a moment of gentle surprise, Clauvère was interrupted in his thoughts by the unexpected presence of Penelope.

She looked up at the stars and whispered, "Beaucoup d'étoiles..." (So many stars.) before turning to meet his eyes.

Clauvère's dark eyes met Penelope's bright blue eyes in a moment of silent connection. Her presence beside him was a soothing balm for his troubled thoughts, and he offered her a soft, appreciative smile. The quiet companionship of the evening, the stars above, and the gentle rustle of leaves created a serene atmosphere that seemed to envelop them both.

Penelope, her usually bound hair cascading gracefully around her shoulders, radiated a sense of calm and understanding. She had an uncanny ability to express herself without words, and in that moment, it felt as if they communicated through unspoken understanding.

With a gentle, wordless gesture, Clauvère shifted slightly, making room for Penelope to lie down beside him. The grass beneath them was cool and comforting, and they lay side by side, their shoulders almost touching. The vast expanse of the starlit sky stretched out above them, casting a quiet, almost enchanted glow over their secluded spot.

As they gazed at the stars, a profound sense of peace washed over them. Clauvère's earlier worries and feelings of displacement began to ebb away in the presence of this kindred spirit. Penelope, for her part, felt a warmth in her heart, knowing that she could offer solace to someone who had also known the sting of loneliness and the harshness of the world.

In the quiet companionship of that Southern evening, Clauvère and Penelope found a moment of respite, a shared understanding that transcended words. They watched the stars twinkle above, their silhouettes framed by the vastness of the universe, and in that serene moment, their individual burdens felt a little lighter.

Their friendship defied the societal norms of the time, for it was a period when prejudices of all kinds were ingrained. Penelope and Clauvère, however, cared not for such divisions; their bond was being forged in the purity of their hearts.

Amidst the vast fields and rustic cottages of the sprawling estate owned by Penelope's family, and it was in the lush green yard of her home that they lay. The scent of wildflowers filled the air, and the gentle rustling of leaves provided the soundtrack to their newly found connection.

Clauvère turned toward Penelope, his expression marked by contemplation. In a soft, tender whisper, he addressed her, "Ma belle, Penny Chanceuse," (My beautiful, Lucky Penny.) a term of endearment that slipped from his lips without premeditation.

To his surprise, Penelope let out a hushed and astonished sound. She averted her gaze from him, her hand instinctively rising to cover her mouth. Clauvère had not anticipated the words, nor did he expect Penelope's immediate response. In the wake of his own blush, he turned away, the unexpected vulnerability leaving him momentarily flustered.

As the seconds passed, he sensed Penelope's hand timidly reaching for his, searching for connection and understanding. It was in this unspoken moment, the interlocking of their fingers, that they found the courage to turn back to one another. Their eyes met, and they shared a smile, a silent communion that spoke volumes about the budding connection between them.

In an uncommon moment, Penelope addressed Clauvère with more than just a single word or two, and to his surprise, it was in French. Despite her slightly imperfect pronunciation, Clauvère found her words easy to comprehend.

"Tu es... mon Clauvère à quatre feuilles," (You are... my four leaf Clauvère.) she said, stumbling only once.

She had rehearsed that line, he realized. The line was too clever, too smooth, for someone who still fumbled over simpler sentences. A bit of wordplay she created with the use of his name.

Clauvère internally clocked that this was more complex than the simple French words she used with his maman. He understood that this was prepared, not spontaneous.

With her free hand, she handed him some things she'd tucked away earlier that afternoon—a token she'd carried since she'd found it in the garden. Penny hadn't initially considered presenting him with it yet, but upon hearing his unprompted confession, she decided to do so.

Her soft hand pressed something cool and delicate into his palm. Only when he brought it closer to the faint lamplight spilling from the house did he see the tiny four-leaf clover.

Clauvère found that he had to blink back tears. "My lucky Penny," he began, his voice tinged with a seriousness that belied his youth, "do you ever wonder about the future?"

Penelope, her blond hair cascading down her shoulders, looked at Clauvère with genuine curiosity. She continued to respond in broken French. "Bien sûr, Clauvère. Qu'est-ce que... tu as dans la tête?" (Of course, Clauvère. What's been on your mind?) she asked, the sentence wobbling as she pieced it together.

Her French was clumsy, the word order strange. He heard what she meant, not the grammar she mangled.

Looking at her, he realized it was her. Perfectly.

Clauvère hesitated, then continued, "Well, I've heard stories of best friends who grow up and get married. Do you think that could happen to us?"

Penelope's eyes widened in surprise, a rosy blush tinting her cheeks. She turned away. Her lips shaped the beginning of an English word—"I ho..."—and then she visibly flinched, swallowing it down.

He noticed that too.

"Je pense... que oui. Peut-être," (I think... yes. Maybe) she corrected, forcing the thought into French instead.

She halted. Her words caught between what she wanted to say and how she thought she should say it. "Les autres... peut-être... ne comprendr—" she paused on the word.

Clauvère gave her the correct pronunciation.

She took a breath, trying again. "Les autres... peut-être... ne comprendraient pas." (The others... perhaps... would not understand."

Clauvère nodded slowly, his gaze fixed on the horizon. Her French was broken but he could understand. "I know, Penny. If we remain here in the colonies, it might be impossible, but think about it. What if we could be by each other's side forever?"

Penelope's voice trembled with effort. "Clauvère... je voudrais... un monde où... c'est possible" (Clauvère... I wish... for a world... it is possible.)

Another pause. She touched the clover between his fingers, choosing each word carefully. "Je... garderai... ce moment... pour toujours." (I... will keep... this moment... forever.)

Penelope struggled with her innermost feelings and the desire to respond honestly to Clauvère's unspoken question. She grappled with the knowledge that they could never openly acknowledge their feelings or be accepted as a couple in the American colonies. As a result, she couldn't simply say "yes" as she wished to.

Clauvère's eyes sparkled with sincerity. "As will I, Penny."

As the first stars began to twinkle in the darkening sky, Penelope and Clauvère carried on their conversation about dreams and hopes. Their words confirming a bond that time and society could not break. Penelope, with her broken French, found Clauvère assisting her in refining her words, while he responded in English.

They knew that their friendship was a treasure and anything more than friendship would face the prejudices of their era. Under the canopy of stars though, Penelope and Clauvère promised to cherish their friendship.

Neither of them knew what the years would demand of them, but for now, under the starry sky and amidst the forgiving night that buzzed and creaked and hoo-ed around them, forever still felt possible.

On the porch of the grand house, Amelia's gaze drifted out into the night, her eyes fixed on the garden below. A smile graced her lips as she witnessed her younger sister's transformation. It seemed like only moments ago that Penelope had clung to their father's coattail, yearning for his attention.

Now, she observed the subtle shift in Penelope's demeanor, a clear sign of her growing independence and a budding sense of self. What hit her the most was hearing her sister's voice, something she had been denied for years. Spoken in broken French as it was, it was the most beautiful thing she had heard in her entire life.

With a sense of pride and a touch of nostalgia, Amelia continued to watch the two of them. She silently admired the bond forming between Penelope and Clauvère, a connection that was quietly reshaping their family dynamics. After a few more minutes of observing, she turned and made her way back into the house, her heart warmed by the sight of Penelope's evolving journey.

Later that night, Penelope sat in front of her vanity, her delicate hands trembling slightly as she held the hairbrush. The soft glow of the candle on the bedside table bathed the room in a warm, golden light. It was time for bed, and her nightly ritual began with brushing her long, platinum-blonde hair. Her locks cascaded down her back in a shimmering waterfall. The scent of lavender and vanilla filled the room.

As she carefully untangled her silken locks, she heard a soft knock on her bedroom door. Penelope knew it was her elder sister, Amelia, who often checked on her. It was a brief, unspoken connection they shared, as Amelia was one of the few people Penelope would interact with in this manner. She paused her brushing and glanced at the door.

Amelia, her elder sister by two years, entered the room and paused in the doorway, her eyes filled with a mix of concern and curiosity. "Penelope," she said softly, "how are you feeling tonight?" She leaned against the door frame, her silhouette softened by the dim light.

Penelope turned her gaze toward Amelia, her expression a mixture of longing and frustration. Penelope knew she couldn't simply respond verbally, but her expressive blue eyes met her sister's, conveying a range of emotions. She offered a small, reassuring smile to Amelia before setting the brush aside and picking up a small notepad and pencil from her vanity.

With careful handwriting, Penelope began to write her response, each letter filled with the trouble of her past.

"I'm okay," she wrote, the pencil gliding across the paper with the familiarity of countless nights. "I'm still adjusting," Penelope's handwriting was neat and precise, a reflection of her meticulous nature. "It's hard, Amelia."

Amelia observed her sister's response, her eyes filled with understanding. She had seen the toll that past events had taken on Penelope. It had been years, and the silence still persisted. The siblings shared a bond that transcended words.

Amelia moved closer, her features showing empathy. "I know it's not easy, especially with the changes since the de La Pointierres arrived."

Penelope nodded in response, her lips forming a faint smile. She appreciated Amelia's words, but her silence was a shield she had carefully constructed, one that separated her from the idea that her words could cause harm.

Amelia, however, noted Penelope's use of the pad and pencil. A question rose to her lips—*earlier, in the garden... had she truly heard her sister's voice?*

It had been so soft, so fleeting, that Amelia wondered whether she had imagined it. But the look on Penelope's face now—the guarded calm, the practiced silence—told her this was not the moment to ask.

So Amelia swallowed the impulse. Whatever had happened outdoors—whatever miracle of voice or courage—belonged to Penelope alone. Amelia would not risk startling her back into silence.

She chose instead to let her sister move at her own pace. It was a magnificent breakthrough, whether spoken of or not, and Amelia decided she would not touch it until Penelope herself reached for it.

With renewed resolve, she reached out and gently squeezed Penelope's shoulder before leaving her to her thoughts. Penelope returned her sister's smile with gratitude.

As the door closed behind her sister, Penelope turned her attention back to the mirror. Her reflection stared back at her, a silent companion in the dimly lit room.

With Amelia's departure, Penelope's thoughts returned to the reason behind her silence. She knew it was time to confront her past, the lingering guilt that held her in its grasp. Penelope had held on to a secret that she had never shared with anyone. The time had come to lay bare the truth that had kept her mute for so long.

She wrote with purpose, her hand moving steadily across the paper as she traced each letter. Her script was elegant and deliberate, much like her revelation.

"I stopped speaking after Mama got sick," she wrote, her heart heavy as she recalled that fateful time. She paused for a moment, the memories vivid in her mind's eye.

The candlelight flickered, casting dancing shadows on the walls, as Penelope continued to write. "I yelled at her, Amelia. I said I wished she wasn't here because she wouldn't play with me. And then she... she went away." The words hung in the air, an unspoken sorrow that had haunted her for years.

As Penelope set down the notepad, a single tear welled up in her eye, glistening in the dim light. She had shared her secret with the silence of the room, and for the first time, the weight on her heart felt a little lighter. The night had become a vessel for her healing, a moment of introspection that she hoped would pave the way for her to find her voice once more.

With a deep breath, Penelope decided to continue to write, her thoughts flowing onto the paper like a secret diary of her emotions and dreams. In this quiet moment, alone with her thoughts, she allowed herself to explore the significance of the nickname "Penny" given to her by Clauvère earlier in the evening.

She wrote, "Penny. It's a simple name, one that feels like a gift. For the first time, I'm seen as more than my silence. Clauvère's eyes held a world of understanding, and when he spoke it, it was as if he'd given me the key to a new world, a world where my voice could exist without causing harm."

In the stillness of the night, surrounded by the comforting scent of her favorite flowers and the soft glow of the candle, Penelope found herself drawn into her own introspection. The onus of her mutism, the pain of her past, and the hope for a different future converged in her thoughts.

Penelope knew that the road ahead would be challenging, but Clauvère's presence had already begun to shape her perception of herself and the world. She couldn't help but wonder if she might, one day, break free from the chains of selective mutism and embrace her true voice, as "Penny."

Penelope and Clauvère
Close from the start

PART TWO

4

The year was now 1771. Winter had come and gone since that memorable night beneath the starry skies. Penny, Clauvère, and Peter, now one year older, had forged an unshakable bond, rooted in their shared history since early childhood. Their connection transcended the boundaries of race and appearances.

On a warm and sunny afternoon, Clauvère, Penny, and Peter found themselves in Penelope's enchanting backyard, an oasis of vibrant flowers, a swing set, and a cozy picnic table where they often indulged in snacks and stories. Today was no different as they engaged in a spirited game of catch, their laughter echoing through the air as they merrily tossed a ball to and fro.

Penelope's father, George, guided Louis through the garden, engrossed in a conversation about upcoming family matters. With patience, Louis observed, sensing a hint of distraction in George's demeanor. Eventually, George mustered a faint smile and opened up about his revelation, "I have something to share, though it may not seem significant, just a family affair, you see."

Louis remained attentive, not wanting to disrupt George's train of thought. George hesitated before revealing the news, "My sister-in-law from England is coming to stay with us. She can be quite challenging to get along with, as she's an extreme... Loyalist. I appreciate how you've never flaunted your nobility, treating me and my daughters as equals. However, Elizabeth firmly believes in maintaining a clear distinction between the classes."

Louis appeared visibly perturbed. One of the driving factors behind his decision to own a plantation in Martinique was his vehement desire to distance himself from his nobility. Long ago, he had departed from his father's estate in the western regions of France, determined to forge his own path. With his own two hands, he had meticulously built his sugar plantation from the ground up. Differing from many of his fellow landowners in the French West Indies, he had chosen to employ a fully compensated labor force, eschewing the institution of slavery.

He adamantly shunned the idea of his title defining him. His aspiration was to be acknowledged for his true self, not merely for his nobility. Taking a deep breath, he finally spoke, "I will make every effort to endure this, but if it becomes overwhelming..." his voice trailed off, the prospect of having to masquerade in a noble role for one person alone already leaving him visibly drained.

In a reassuring gesture, George extended his hand, resting it gently on Louis's shoulder. "Thank you, my friend. I can only ask that you endure it as best as you can." The strength of their friendship, though tested, remained a constant source of support.

George decided to change both his approach and the subject of their conversation. Recognizing the close integration of their families, despite the absence of formal bonds, he believed discussing family matters would serve as a pleasant diversion.

"So, how's Minuette doing?" George inquired, hoping to initiate a discussion about her progress in mastering English.

Louis chuckled in response. His wife had been under Amelia's tutelage for quite a while, but her grasp of the language remained somewhat elusive. She preferred conversing in French, particularly with Penny, who had swiftly embraced the language. Minuette had taken it upon herself to ensure that the young girl mastered French before fully delving into English with Amelia.

As a result, Amelia found herself with more free time. She was currently being courted by a young man from one of Savannah's prominent families, and her attention was wholly absorbed by that endeavor. Now that Penny had become more fluent in French, Minuette had taken on the role of educating both Penny and Clauvère. Curiously, Peter's parents had also begun to see the value in their son learning French, leading him to occasionally join the lessons, creating a unique dynamic in their shared educational journey.

While Peter's family had become acquainted with the de La Pointierre and Hartford families through Peter's relationships with their children, their connection wasn't as close. The demands of running their cotton mill absorbed much of their time, which led Peter to spend a significant amount of his free time at the de La Pointierre residence. Peter's family paid no mind to the fact that the de La Pointierre household was mixed, with Louis being a Count from France, Minuette being of mixed Caribbean birth and their son, Clauvère being a mulatto.

Peter confided in both Penny and Clauvère about the reactions he faced at his regular school. The headmaster, in particular, voiced his disapproval of Peter learning from Minuette, citing her racial background, although he couldn't argue too strenuously since she was the sole effective French teacher in the city.

The headmaster tolerated the knowledge of Minuette's instruction due to her exceptional fluency, another reason for his acceptance was her noble status as a potential Countess, which carried significant weight in their society. However, this did not extend to Clauvère being included among the classmates of white students at the school house. Fortunately, this arrangement suited everyone well since Clauvère was now satisfactorily being tutored by Amelia along side of Penny.

George and Louis returned to the Hartford residence, proceeding into the parlor where they resumed their previous conversation.

George began to confide in Louis about the more personal aspects of his relationship with his sister-in-law, Elizabeth. He shared details about her journey from England and the reasons behind her impending arrival, which would soon see her integrated into the Hartford family.

"The girls are truly remarkable and are growing into fine young women," George remarked, expressing his pride in his daughters. "However, I believe they require a more... feminine influence to complete their upbringing. With their mother's untimely passing, I fear that I lack the necessary qualities to provide them with the guidance they need, being, well, not a woman myself."

Louis chuckled at George. "Indeed, I'm quite certain of that," he quipped, raising his brandy snifter in a playful salute before taking a sip.

George nodded in agreement, his concern for his daughter's future palpable. "The landed gentry in this city is every bit as burdensome to contend with as it was in England."

In the colonies, money did not smell like sugar—it smelled like cotton.

Louis had never planned to trade sugar for cotton. But since arriving in Savannah, the idea had followed him—at dinners, in contracts, in the mouths of men who spoke of land as if it were destiny. Those thoughts closed out with a gentle smile as he glanced back over at George.

George turned to Louis, curiosity evident in his gaze. "I'm certain the nobility in France can be just as vexing, if not more so."

Louis, reflecting on his own experiences, replied thoughtfully, "Indeed, it was precisely the stifling obligations of nobility in France that prompted me to leave and start anew in Martinique. The rigid expectations and limited freedom to pursue one's passions pushed me to forge my own path. I left, bringing my younger brother with me, and decided to leave my mark on the world by establishing a sugar plantation."

George swiftly grasped the significance of Louis's decision, which had set the stage for their current success. "I'm forever grateful that fate brought us together."

Louis shared the sentiment, contemplating the outcome of his choices, which had ultimately led him to his beloved treasure and wife, Minuette, and, in turn, blessed him with a remarkable son, Clauvère. He realized that he wouldn't alter a single decision that had led to this beautiful outcome.

Their conversation then turned to George's sister-in-law, who was meant to assume the role of providing the girls with a woman's education. Louis inquired, "So, is your sister-in-law stepping in to fill the void left by your late wife, ensuring the girls receive proper guidance?"

George nodded solemnly. "Yes, recent events have compelled me to make this decision. With Amelia approaching a certain age and courting that young man from the Waverly family, I worry about her acceptance. After all, my family is just commoners with some wealth, nothing more."

Louis understood the depth of George's concern and empathized with his desire to secure the best possible future for his daughters in a society that often placed great importance on social standing.

Louis nodded in understanding. "It's a difficult decision, but one made out of genuine concern for your daughters' well-being. Having your sister-in-law Elizabeth here to provide a woman's guidance is a thoughtful choice. It ensures that the girls receive the proper upbringing they deserve, especially in a society that often places significant emphasis on such matters."

George sighed, his worries still etched on his face. "You're absolutely right, Louis. My daughters mean the world to me, and I want to give them every advantage in life. But it's not just about society; it's about their happiness and prospects. Amelia's suitor, young Mr. Waverly, comes from a family that values their lineage. I fear that our modest background might not sit well with them."

Louis placed a reassuring hand on George's shoulder. "George, you've built a successful life for yourself and your family here in Savannah. You've gained the respect and admiration of many, including myself. It's not just about lineage or titles; it's about the character and values instilled in your daughters. I have no doubt that with your guidance and Elizabeth's, they will grow into remarkable young women."

George's expression softened as he looked at his friend. "Thank you, Louis. Your support means the world to me. It's a comfort to know that we're in this together, facing life's challenges side by side."

Louis smiled warmly. "Indeed, my friend. We've come a long way from our past, and I have no doubt that our families will thrive, even in the face of societal expectations."

George, however, remained unaltered in demeanor following his recent exchange with Louis. An air of somberness still hung about him, suggesting that something deeper troubled his thoughts. Louis, ever perceptive, sensed this lingering unease and inquired about the source of George's continued distress. They had already explored his concerns about Amelia's impending marriage age, the upbringing of his daughters, and the purpose of his sister-in-law's presence. Louis couldn't fathom what else might be causing George's anxiety.

"What else is weighing on your mind, George?" Louis queried, his concern evident. "Our previous discussions don't seem to have alleviated your worries."

George responded with a faint smile, hinting at the complexities he had yet to reveal. "There are... complications associated with my sister-in-law, Elizabeth, coming to live with my family."

Louis awaited further elaboration but received none, prompting him to coax George into divulging more. "Please, go on."

George took a deep breath and exhaled audibly. "When we were children back in England, I grew up with my late wife, Regina, and her sister, Elizabeth. I fell in love with Regina and eventually married her. However, Elizabeth had confessed her feelings for me before our marriage, while we were still quite young. I couldn't reciprocate her affections, citing my love for her sister."

Louis hummed in understanding, acknowledging the complex history.

"Elizabeth married after Regina and I departed for the American colonies," George continued, "but her husband has since passed away, just as Regina has. Elizabeth, staying in touch with us, was aware of this. Since then, she's persisted in expressing her feelings, and I've continued to reject her advances."

"I can see how this might create an awkward situation," Louis commented. "So she comes here to your home in the American colonies, not only to educate her nieces but also to try to sway your affections."

George nodded, his gaze fixed on the brandy snifter he held tightly in both hands, his shoulders slumping forward. "That's the crux of the matter," he admitted. "I have no desire to enter into marriage again. My sole objective is to provide the best for my daughters."

Louis began to grasp the broader scope of George's concerns. While he was genuinely worried about his friend's current stress, he recognized that there was little he could actively do to alleviate the situation. Nonetheless, he could extend his support, and that's precisely what he offered.

"I understand your concerns, George, and they do seem valid," Louis empathized. "I think you should keep your focus on the objectives of Elizabeth's presence within your family. She has the potential to exert a substantial positive influence on the girls' lives, guiding them toward womanhood."

Louis paused, considering how he might further address the issue of Elizabeth's affections for George. He then articulated his thoughts aloud. "Regarding your sister-in-law's feelings, my suggestion would be to continue communicating with her consistently and firmly, conveying your true sentiments. I believe she will eventually come to understand."

A faint smile crept onto George's face as he leaned back in his seat, glancing out of the parlor window at the sun's radiant beams. He let out a light laugh and turned his attention back to Louis, his humor returning. "You have no idea how exasperatingly persistent that woman can be. She's far too reminiscent of her late sister in that regard."

Resolved to heed Louis's advice and address the matter head-on, George allowed their conversation to shift to other topics, setting aside the complexities of Elizabeth's arrival for the moment.

The morning sun painted the Savannah sky in strokes of pink and gold, the promise of heat already shimmering over the horizon. Within the La Pointierre estate, the day began not with idleness but with quiet purpose.

Silk whispered and buckles clicked as Louis and Minuette prepared for the day ahead. He adjusted the cuffs of his coat with the practiced precision of habit, though his gaze lingered on the window rather than the mirror. She fastened her earrings without hurry, her reflection calm but distant, the faintest smile curving when their eyes met across the room.

When they descended the grand staircase, light spilled through the high windows, gilding the dark wood beneath their steps. Clauvère waited below, his posture already betraying a young man's eagerness to be older than his years, Peter beside him shifting his weight with the restless patience of a friend caught in someone else's family morning.

"It will be a long day," Louis said quietly, glancing toward the window. "But if the land is half as promising as they say, it will be worth the miles."

Minuette adjusted one of his cuffs, smiling faintly. "You always see promise where others see dust."

"And you," he replied, "always remind me what's worth keeping."

"Then let's go see what's waiting," she said.

The sound of their carriage approaching signaled the start of a day that would see them explore the pristine lands around Savannah and delve into the world of cotton cultivation. Their dreams and ambitions were woven into the fabric of this day, and as they stepped outside to greet their awaiting carriage, the possibilities stretched out before them, ready to be discovered.

Louis turned to his son, Clauvère, and addressed him with a firm yet caring tone. "Clauvère, your mother and I are exploring the lands beyond the city. During our absence, we have arranged for you to spend the day with George and his family at their estate. This way, you'll have some company and activities to keep you engaged."

Clauvère's face lit up with a warm and affectionate smile as he bid farewell to his parents. With a heartfelt expression, he watched them make their way to the awaiting carriage, knowing that his own carriage would follow closely behind.

The sun bathed the fertile land around Savannah, Georgia, in a warm, golden light. Chevalier Louis de La Pointierre and his wife, Minuette, strolled through the open fields, their steps light and eager. It was a beautiful morning, and the possibilities stretched out before them, as vast as the unending horizon.

As they walked, they gazed upon the land they were considering for purchase. The rich, fertile soil held promise, and the cotton fields, though yet to be sown, seemed like a canvas waiting to be painted. Louis was filled with the air of authority, while Minuette's grace and beauty remained a constant presence by his side.

"It's good land," he said, scanning the horizon. "Flat, rich, near the river. You could build almost anything here."

Minuette smiled faintly, shading her eyes with one hand.

"You're already building it in your head, aren't you?"

Louis glanced at her, a small grin tugging at his mouth.

"Perhaps. It would be fine to have something of our own here—something that belongs to more than sugar."

She looked out over the open fields again.

"If it gives our son a steadier future, I suppose I can learn to love cotton too."

As they continued to walk, their dreams flowed freely, painting a picture of their future. Louis spoke with enthusiasm,

"If we start here, it could be something lasting," he said. "Clauvère could build upon it one day—something of his own."

Minuette nodded in agreement, her heart swelling with hope.

"You always think of him first," she said softly. "It's good. He deserves to have something steadier than we began with."

Louis's smile lingered, eyes following the line of the distant trees.

"Then let's see what this place can give us."

Their words echoed with ambition and optimism as they wandered through the untouched fields. This land was not only a symbol of future wealth but also of the legacy they intended to leave for their beloved son, Clauvère.

They shared a vision, a dream of success and growth, of building a future for their family in this new world. As they continued their walk, they remained blissfully unaware of the darker realities of the cotton industry, for their hearts were filled with hope and the promise of a bright future.

With their plans set, Louis and Minuette made their way back to their waiting carriage. The day's agenda still had one more destination, a local cotton plantation. Their primary aim was to gain a deeper understanding of the cotton industry, particularly the latter stages of production. Louis had taken care of the necessary arrangements, securing permission from the plantation owner for their visit. Eager anticipation filled the carriage as it rolled along, the couple keen to unravel the mysteries that lay ahead.

As Minuette sat in the comfortable carriage, the rolling countryside of Savannah passing by, her thoughts turned inward, weaving a tapestry of contemplation and reflection. The prospect of a new life in the American colonies had filled her heart with a mixture of anticipation and uncertainty. Her transition had been a far cry from her native French West Indies, and she couldn't help but recall the occasional challenges she had encountered since their arrival.

She pondered her husband, Louis, and the deep love he had for both her and their son, Clauvère. The warmth of his affection was a comforting constant in her life. His unwavering support and shared dreams had been their guiding star, and she was grateful for his presence in every step of their journey.

Her thoughts also drifted to Clauvère, their beloved son, whose happiness and success were the compass of her world. The joy she found in motherhood was a profound source of strength and purpose. As her thoughts drifted and turned to him, she recalled scenes of him chatting and laughing with the young girl Penny, a gentle smile played upon her lips. She was delighted to see the blossoming friendship between the two children, their innocent laughter and camaraderie bringing warmth to her heart.

There was also the consideration of Penny herself. Penny's selective mutism had posed an initial challenge, but over time, they had managed to forge a connection. Early on, Penny had started directing her focus towards Minuette during breaks from her lessons. Minuette attributed this bond to Penny's longing for a motherly figure, having lost her own at a tender age.

This realization had prompted Minuette to adopt a gentle and reassuring tone when speaking to Penny, and it had been a delightful surprise whenever Penny occasionally ventured to repeat a word or two in French during their private interactions. Now, Minuette observed that Penny had become more expressive, freely conversing in French with both her and Clauvère, eliminating the need for the notepad she had previously clung to as her only means of communication.

Despite the challenges and the vast unknown that lay ahead, she felt a sense of unity and purpose within her family. Their journey into the American colonies might be filled with surprises, but with Louis's love, her maternal devotion, and the bonds forming between Clauvère and Penny, she believed they could navigate any path together.

As the carriage approached the plantation, the sun began its descent, casting a rich, golden glow upon the sprawling fields that stretched before them. The journey came to a halt atop a hill, affording them a breathtaking view of the cotton plantation below. Minuette had expressed her desire to take in this magnificent panorama before proceeding to the manor house and meeting the landowner.

At the precipice of the extensive plantation, Louis and his wife, Minuette, were confronted with a scene that defied their expectations.

Both Louis and Minuette cast their discerning gazes upon the land, each driven by their unique motivations. Louis, with eyes darkened by a glimmer of curiosity, harbored ambitions of expanding their holdings into the American colonies. The enticing rumors of cotton cultivation had piqued his interest, promising wealth in the cotton trade and luring them to this place.

Minuette, exuding elegance and poise, stood by her husband's side. In her native French West Indies, she and Louis had presided over a flourishing sugar plantation, where the air was saturated with the fragrance of sugarcane, and laborers toiled beneath the tropical sun. However, nothing could have prepared them for the stark reality that unfolded below the hill they now surveyed.

Their gazes shifted as they watched the African slaves working the cotton fields. It was a sight neither of them had encountered before. The men and women bent low to the earth, their hands picking the fluffy white tufts of cotton. Their fingertips enduring the sting of the barbed stems in the process. Louis had seen his share of laborers, but there was something profoundly unsettling about the scene before him.

Minuette, too, was taken aback. She had never been exposed to the institution of slavery as it was in the American colonies. In the French West Indies, their laborers were indentured workers, bound by contracts, and though far from ideal, it was a world apart from the brutal chattel slavery that she saw now.

Louis cleared his throat, his voice heavy with a mixture of disquiet and disapproval. "This is not what I expected, Minuette. The tales of cotton's riches did not mention this."

Minuette's gaze remained fixed on the laborers, her heart heavy with empathy for the plight of those in the fields. "No, Louis, it did not. I had heard rumors, but I had not truly comprehended the extent of this... cruelty."

They continued to watch in silence as the overseer cracked his whip, and the laborers toiled under the setting sun. The land might promise riches, but at what cost? It was a moral reckoning, and it weighed heavily on both their souls.

As they turned away from the cotton fields, a silent understanding passed between them. They had come seeking wealth, but they could not profit from the exploitation they had witnessed. Their principles and their consciences stood in the way.

As Louis and Minuette stood at the precipice, overlooking the sprawling cotton fields, an indomitable hush settled between them. Minuette's grip on Louis's arm subtly tightened, a silent plea for comfort in the face of the harsh reality unfolding below. The morning sun bathed the land in a golden glow, but Minuette's sigh, soft and almost imperceptible, betrayed the heaviness in her heart.

Her hands, clasped together, fingers entwining, betrayed the turmoil within. A furrow appeared on her brow, her usually composed expression faltering, revealing her profound thought and empathy. Her gaze occasionally averted, as if unable to bear the stark sight. Though she stood poised, she couldn't help but unconsciously touch the back of her own hand, as if considering the implications of the skin she lived in. Seeking solace, she moved closer to Louis, the disturbing tableau below leaving a profound mark on her, tears unshed but glistening in her eyes.

Louis cast a compassionate gaze upon his wife, her visage fraught with evident distress, and he comprehended the source of her disquiet. Minuette's forays into the American colonies had been scant, her ventures seldom extending beyond the confines of their Savannah estate.

Yet even within those limited interactions, she had experienced instances of discrimination. He noticed the fleeting glance she cast at the back of her own hand in that moment, a silent, poignant reminder of the shade of her own skin. It was an act that resonated with the understanding that, in the eyes of others, she too was grouped with those toiling in the fields below.

Louis took Minuette's hand, and they walked away from the cotton plantation, their decision clear. They would not go into the cotton industry, for the price of wealth should never be the suffering of others. Especially not based on the color of their skin. Their noble hearts remained uncorrupted, and they would find their fortune through more honorable means.

In that moment, they turned their backs on the cotton fields, carrying with them the knowledge that some riches were not worth pursuing.

As spring continued to unfold its vibrant tapestry over Savannah, the tension in the Hartford estate seemed to blossom alongside the flowers. The gentle warmth in the air was at odds with the simmering unease within the household. In the midst of it all, a new presence had arrived to add another layer of complexity to the family dynamics.

Elizabeth Salisbury, Penelope's stern and traditional aunt, had come to stay. Her arrival was heralded by a flurry of whispered conversations and nervous glances exchanged among the household staff. Elizabeth, a woman of a certain age, with graying hair neatly pinned up and a penchant for lace-trimmed dresses, had very particular views on propriety and social decorum.

Penelope Hartford's life took an unexpected turn when her aunt arrived to live with them. Elizabeth was her mother's sister, and her arrival was heralded as an opportunity to teach the sisters the proper ways of young ladies. However, her presence stirred complex dynamics within the Hartford family.

Amelia and Penelope, dressed impeccably and filled with anticipation, waited in the parlor of their home. They stood with the proper deference, ready to greet their aunt as she made her way through the grand house. George, with an air of courteous guidance, led her through the rooms. He couldn't help but notice the critical glances she cast upon the staff, the disapproving huffs at the decor, and the general aura of dissatisfaction that seemed to radiate from her, leaving an impact on his household staff.

As the impromptu "tour" continued, George made a concerted effort to keep his own displeasure in check, even though the presence of his sister-in-law in his home was trying. He took a deep breath, attempting to quell the rising discomfort he felt.

In this brief moment of respite, he wrestled with the thought that perhaps giving in to her suggestions and inviting her had been a mistake. However, with her having relinquished her possessions in England, including her late husband's home, she had nowhere else to go if George were to turn her away. His guilt gnawed at him, leaving him conflicted about the situation.

George Hartford, a widower himself, had been initially hesitant about Elizabeth's stay. She was persistent, insisting that her help was necessary. While George was aware of her desire to become his wife, he was equally aware of her traditional views and unwavering loyalty to the English Crown. He had reservations about getting into a relationship with someone whose values were so different from his own.

Elizabeth entered the parlor, her gaze sweeping over Amelia and Penelope with an air of disapproval. She couldn't mask her dissatisfaction, and her demeanor seemed to ooze a subtle superiority. She blamed their perceived shortcomings on what she saw as a lack of proper female guidance, a critique aimed squarely at George's parenting.

"Amelia, Penelope," she began, her voice stern, "it's quite evident that you've been raised without the guidance of a proper woman. It's time for things to change now that I've arrived."

Amelia exchanged a quick, uneasy glance with Penelope. They knew that their aunt's arrival would bring changes, but they had yet to grasp the full extent.

Elizabeth turned her attention to George, her brother-in-law, with a look that suggested she found his parenting skills severely lacking. "George," she addressed him, "I can see you've done your best, but it's clear that a woman's touch has been missing from their upbringing. You've allowed them to grow up rough shod without a mother's guidance. They need discipline to rein them in from their wild ways.

George, although unsettled by the criticism, kept his composure and remained silent. As he observed Elizabeth and her interactions with her nieces, George couldn't help but wonder how she could form such swift and seemingly judgmental assumptions about their behavior. It had been such a brief meeting, and he found it hard to believe that she could discern their true character in such a short span of time.

"Now, girls," Elizabeth continued, returning her gaze to Amelia and Penelope, "things will be different from now on. There are rules to follow in this house, and you'll abide by them. First and foremost, you will address me as 'Aunt Elizabeth,' and I expect to be shown proper respect. Secondly, we will focus on cultivating those feminine virtues that are so desperately lacking in your upbringing."

Amelia and Penelope exchanged glances once more, both feeling their aunt's expectations and wondering what lay ahead in this new chapter of their lives.

The next few days proved to be quite tumultuous for everyone as Elizabeth's presence loomed large in the house. Within just a day, George was approached by two of his household staff who informed him that they would no longer continue working on his estate. They requested a settlement of their wages and a letter of recommendation for their future employment.

George felt alarmed and disheartened by these sudden changes in his household. The most concerning revelation occurred on the first night of her arrival when he and Elizabeth were in the parlor. She learned about Amelia's romantic involvement with the Waverly boy and her role as a tutor for the younger children, Penelope and Clauvère.

Elizabeth and George sat in the dimly lit parlor that first night, her disapproval hanging heavily in the air. She couldn't hide the disdain in her eyes as she glanced at George.

"George, I must say I find it rather distressing that Amelia has taken it upon herself to act as a tutor. At her age, she should be focusing on more ladylike pursuits," Elizabeth remarked with a hint of condescension.

George raised an eyebrow, his patience waning. "Amelia's always shown a keen mind. She enjoys teaching and has a natural talent for it. I see no harm in encouraging her interests."

Elizabeth's frown deepened. "And what about this Waverly boy? I hear she's allowed him to court her, with your permission. It's wholly inappropriate for a girl of her age to be involved in such matters."

George's voice remained calm, but a touch of irritation seeped in. "Amelia is a young woman now, and she deserves the chance to explore relationships and find love."

Inwardly, Elizabeth seethed, thinking to herself that she needed to intervene and gain control over the two girls. If she could assert herself successfully, perhaps she could win George's affections and influence the direction of the household.

George observed Elizabeth's disapproval but remained steadfast in his response. "Amelia is responsible and mature for her age. I trust her judgment, and we should let her explore these feelings. After all, she's at the age where girls marry."

Elizabeth's lips tightened, her frustration growing. "George, it's important that the girls have proper guidance. I'm here to provide that guidance. It's clear they've been lacking it."

George's tone remained measured as he responded, "I appreciate your concern, Elizabeth, but I've raised them to the best of my ability since their mother's passing. They're good girls. I believe we can find a way to balance your guidance with the freedom they've had so far."

Elizabeth pondered her next move. She needed to find a way to exert her influence without alienating George. Winning his affections was a challenging task, but one she was determined to pursue.

The next day Elizabeth took the opportunity to gather Amelia and Penelope in the drawing room, her demeanor as stern as ever. It was time to impart the knowledge and values she deemed essential to transform the girls into proper young ladies. She had always believed in the importance of decorum, etiquette, and grace.

"Girls," she began, her voice crisp and authoritative, "it's high time you receive the education you've been lacking in terms of proper etiquette and decorum. The first lesson I intend to teach you is how to carry yourselves with grace and poise. You should always walk with a straight back, shoulders held back, and your heads held high. Remember, the way you present yourselves reflects not only upon you but also upon your family."

Amelia and Penelope exchanged a knowing glance, aware that their aunt's arrival would usher in a period of change. Elizabeth continued, "Furthermore, you must master the art of conversation. This includes not just what you say but how you say it. You should speak clearly, with confidence, and always in a respectful manner. It's crucial to listen attentively when others speak, showing that you value their words."

The girls nodded, taking in their aunt's words. Elizabeth's gaze bore into them as she laid down her expectations. "You'll also be taught the intricacies of proper dining etiquette. There are rules for every aspect of a meal, from the use of utensils to the way you engage in conversation. You must learn to adapt to various social situations and conduct yourselves appropriately."

Amelia and Penelope absorbed their aunt's guidance with a mixture of trepidation and curiosity. They knew that adapting to Elizabeth's teachings would be challenging, but they also recognized that these lessons were an essential part of their growth into young women. Elizabeth's arrival marked a significant shift in their lives, one that held the promise of personal growth and refinement, even if it also brought conflict and tension.

However, the tension in the household became more palpable the day that Elizabeth met the son of the de La Pointierre family, who were close friends and frequent visitors.

Clauvère felt a growing void in his routine. He hadn't seen Penny or Amelia in two days and had been missing Amelia's tutoring. He decided to discuss his concerns with his parents.

When he brought it up, Louis explained that the arrival of their Aunt Elizabeth had disrupted their daily routine. Despite this explanation, even Louis was unsure, as George hadn't provided a clear reason for the interruption in Amelia's instruction or the absence of the girls' visits to the de La Pointierre estate in the past few days.

Clauvère asked his parents if he could call upon the Hartfords and afford them a visit as a result of the disruption of the routine that had been established. They granted his request.

It took an extra day before Clauvère could finally reunite with the girls. Adhering to the norms of polite society, he first sent a formal request, outlining his intent to visit. It wasn't until the following day that he received a response from George. Filled with excitement and anticipation, he rode in the carriage, eagerly looking forward to reuniting with Penny and Amelia.

Penelope with her sister Amelia

The Hartford sisters

5

Clauvère's arrival at the Hartford estate was a surprise to Elizabeth, who had not been appraised of his visit. George had failed to mention this scheduled visit to her on his way out to the office that morning, never having had the need to do so because of a lack of any other adult in the house to consider.

Clauvère was waiting at the entryway inside the grand hall of the house as a servant went to announce his arrival to Elizabeth who was in the drawing room with the girls, teaching them knitting.

"Madam Salisbury, young Chevalier Clauvère Jean-Claude de La Pointierre has arrived," a servant informed Elizabeth, using Clauvère's full given name and title. Elizabeth was perturbed that the arrival was unexpected. She was also excited at the arrival of someone of nobility to her doorstep and the esteem that she believed such a person's visit could bring her.

Amelia and Penny exchanged surprised glances. Clauvère's unexpected visit had taken them aback, but they couldn't hide their excitement. However, as they took a moment to ponder the situation, a new realization crept in. Elizabeth had yet to meet any of the de La Pointierre family members, and that presented the potential for complications. Curious and slightly apprehensive, the girls wondered how this encounter would unfold.

Elizabeth's heart quickened as the servant announced the arrival of "Chevalier Clauvère Jean-Claude de La Pointierre." She repeated the name to herself, delighting in it the way others delighted in famous stage actors, pianists maybe, or crowned heads — a brush with a world she revered from afar.

Her eyes sparkled with a subtle glint of anticipation. The name itself carried an air of nobility, and she couldn't help but feel a surge of excitement at the prospect of hosting someone of such esteemed lineage.

With every step she took out of the drawing room, her breath held a touch of expectation. The very idea that a nobleman had crossed her threshold awakened a sense of pride in her — a sense that she was now part of a world she had long admired from afar. She carried this newfound dignity quietly, hidden in her gaze. It was concealed in the poised smile that graced her lips, allowing the mere presence of nobility to speak volumes about her own sense of honor and privilege.

Elizabeth walked briskly toward the entryway, her excitement barely contained. She failed to notice that she had been followed during her departure by Amelia and Penny. The thought of how the young nobleman Clauvère's visit was a cause for both anticipation and anxiety for Elizabeth, so such inattention was to be expected.

Shortly Elizabeth entered the grand hall. As she approached, she saw his back, the posture of a noble. Without hesitation, she curtsied and began her greeting, her voice polished and her words respectful.

"Chevalier de La Pointierre, it is an honor to make your acquaintance," she began with a warm smile. "I trust your journey here was without incident. Please, come in and make yourself—"

Her words hung in the air, unfinished, as Clauvère turned to face her. The sight that met her eyes was unexpected, and it struck her like a bolt of lightning. Elizabeth's polite demeanor froze, and her gaze locked onto the young boy before her, a realization dawning upon her like a harsh truth. Clauvère was a black boy of just fourteen years or so. The shock, a reflection of the era and societal views, rippled across her features, momentarily robbing her of words.

Elizabeth turned to the servant who had come with her to the door. "Why is this negro here?" she demanded. "Where is the young lord, Clauvère Jean-Claude de La Pointierre?"

The servant looked at Elizabeth in confusion. He pointed. "Madam, this *is* Chevalier Clauvère Jean-Claude de La Pointierre."

The room fell into silence as she grappled with the implications of this revelation. Her mind raced, and the dissonance between her preconceived notions and the reality before her left her momentarily breathless. The elegant parlor with tea serving the nobility she had imagined, all blurred and faded away as she faced the unyielding truth that stood before her.

Elizabeth's obliviousness was concealed as Amelia and Penny stepped forward to greet Clauvère. She remained in stunned silence, observing their heartfelt reunion after their time apart.

"Clauvère," Amelia called out as she embraced him, planting kisses on both his cheeks. Penny was right beside them.

Penny and Amelia shifted positions after Amelia greeted Clauvère. The unspoken connection between Penny and Clauvère was evident to any observer. It was not merely a matter of changing places; Penny's actions revealed a deeper bond with Clauvère. She spoke to him in French in soft whispers, the words unintelligible to Elizabeth, but the emotions behind them were unmistakable.

Although Elizabeth had only been in the house for four days, the fact that she had yet to hear the youngest of her nieces utter a single word finally struck her. The shock of her delayed realization washed over her, leaving her astounded at her own lack of observation. It had taken her four days to notice something that should have been evident within the first day at most.

Elizabeth couldn't contain her mounting frustration and, interrupting the warm exchange between Penny, Amelia, and Clauvère, she admonished the girls sternly. "Amelia, Penelope, enough of this display! You are young ladies, and I expect you to behave with the proper decorum befitting your station. Show some restraint and remember the rules of our household." The abrupt shift in her tone sent a palpable tension through the room. The joy of their reunion was swiftly replaced by an atmosphere of strained obedience as the girls moved to stand behind Elizabeth.

Elizabeth tugged gently on her blouse, exaggerating the straightening of her posture by pushing her shoulders back and tilting her head, allowing her to look down her nose at Clauvère. She began, "Look here, boy. I don't know who you are —" but was swiftly cut off by Clauvère's raised hand. Her body quickly shifted back.

Frustrations he had suppressed over racial slurs said behind his back, the snubs, gazes, whispers, and the recent incident in the store with the proprietor all reached a breaking point, ignited by Elizabeth's slight and her condescending tone.

Clauvère opened the door to the front of the house and called out, "Thibault, soyez présent!" (Thibault, attend!)

Amelia and Penny exchanged concerned glances, their faces mirroring the confusion written across Elizabeth's. They couldn't comprehend what was unfolding.

A moment later, Thibault entered the house and offered a bow of respect before Clauvère. He inquired, "Oui, chevalier Clauvère. De quoi avez-vous besoin, Mon Seigneur?" (Yes, Chevalier Clauvère. What do you need, My Lord?)

Clauvère, maintaining a calm expression, turned and extended his hand in Elizabeth's direction. "Si cette femme parle encore et m'insulte, ouvre-lui la gorge avec ton épée," (If this woman speaks again and insults me, open her throat with your sword.) he instructed with a stern tone.

Thibault stole a brief glance at the boy who had issued such a startling directive. His face remained passive, still. Thibault mirrored that look, unfazed by the gravity of his lord's command. Clauvère's words were delivered with an unsettling absence of emotion, adding an extra layer of disquiet to the situation. Instinctively, Thibault's hand drifted towards the hilt of his sword as he locked his gaze onto Elizabeth, fully prepared for any potential insult aimed at his master.

It took only a few moments for Penny to realize what Clauvère had just commanded with the dispassionate look on his face and the dead eyes she saw. She screamed as she moved past her aunt to Clauvère. "Non non, Mon Seigneur. S'il vous plaît, ne le faites pas. Pour mon bien, s'il te plaît." (No, no, My Lord. Please don't do it. For my sake, please.)

The words tumbled out in a rush, and although Amelia had only a basic grasp of French, she comprehended more than Elizabeth. She sensed the gravity of the situation, recognizing that something perilous had transpired between Clauvère and Thibault. It became evident that only Penny's heartfelt pleas had the potential to sway the course of events.

Clauvère seethed with anger, the rushing of blood in his ears almost drowning out Penny's words. However, her next words struck him on a level he hadn't anticipated. Until that moment, their unspoken sentiments had not been conveyed in words by either of them.

Penny's mind raced as she pleaded with Clauvère to reconsider. She couldn't bear the thought of him taking such drastic action. It was a dangerous command, and her heart ached at the realization of the consequences it might bring. But it was more than that; it was also a moment of acknowledging the depth of her feelings for him.

"Mon Seigneur, je t'aime," (My Lord, I love you.) Penny blurted out, her words hurried and intense. She stopped, startled by her own words.

Then, in a softer, more deliberate tone, she repeated, "Je t'aime. Je ne peux pas te laisser faire ça. Si vous, Mon Seigneur, m'aimez, alors s'il vous plaît, réfléchissez à votre décision." (I love you. I can't let you do this. If you, My Lord, love me, then please reconsider.)

Tears welled up in her eyes and began to cascade down her cheeks. She had never been so vulnerable, never laid her heart bare in such a way.

Clauvère, struggling to hold back his own tears, enveloped Penny in a warm embrace, pulling her closer. With a gesture, he signaled Thibault to leave the house. "Je fais cela uniquement pour toi et par amour pour toi," (I do this only for your sake and my love for you.) he whispered as he wiped the tears away from her swollen eyes.

This marked Penny's first acknowledgment of Chevalier Clauvère's nobility; she had always known him simply as 'Clauvère,' neither more nor less.

The room filled with tense, hushed moments, as no one dared to disrupt the connection between Penny and Clauvère. Eventually, Penny reached out, taking Clauvère's hand, and led him to the drawing room. Clauvère shot a warning glance at Elizabeth, sending a shiver down her spine. In silence, Elizabeth observed their departure, unaware of the details but instinctively aware that they had just averted a potentially dangerous situation. She silently thanked Penny for whatever words had diffused the tension between her and Clauvère.

Clauvère and Penny found solace in each other's presence, sitting closely on the settee in the drawing room. The tumultuous events of a few moments ago were now but a distant memory. As they sat there, their hands entwined, the residual tension from that incident gradually ebbed away, leaving their hearts to beat in perfect harmony.

The drawing room enveloped them in an atmosphere of tranquility. Soft, muted sunlight filtered through the heavy, velvet curtains, casting a warm, gentle glow upon the room's elegant furnishings. The air carried a faint scent of antique wood, well-worn leather, and a hint of lavender, invoking a sense of timeless comfort.

In the background, the subtle ticking of an antique clock on the mantel provided a steady, reassuring rhythm, while the occasional chirping of the birds outside the window added a soft, melodic undertone. The room seemed to echo with the hushed whispers of history, as if the walls held secrets of generations past.

As they sat together, Penny and Clauvère felt the room's calming embrace, allowing their worries to slowly dissipate. With each breath, they found respite in the serene, ageless ambiance, their connection deepening amidst the subtle symphony of sights, sounds, and scents that surrounded them.

Clauvère focused his thoughts, determined to quell the anger that had welled up within him. It was an anger ignited by the unsettling encounter with Penny's aunt, Elizabeth, who had flagrantly crossed boundaries, pushing Clauvère to the brink of his patience in dealing with the pervasive discrimination he faced due to the color of his skin.

"I am the descendant of a Count," Clauvère reminded himself. "But I am first and foremost a human being deserving of respect. I will not allow these prejudices to define me."

Yet, this personal mantra alone couldn't fully soothe the ache in his heart. It was the presence of the girl beside him that had helped him quell the seething anger that had clouded his judgment to the extent of contemplating dire actions, such as instructing his attendant, Thibault, to take drastic measures should Elizabeth utter another disparaging word.

He was acutely aware of the repercussions stemming from his recent actions. Although there was no physical bloodshed within the Hartford estate's entryway, violence had indeed occurred – a violence of words with far-reaching consequences. It had stirred in Clauvère a profound realization of how determined he was to assert his existence.

Turning to his side, Clauvère gazed upon Penny. Her head rested against his shoulder, her eyes tightly shut. If he didn't know better, he might have assumed she was asleep, but the tears actively coursing down her cheeks revealed the truth behind the façade. She was neither slumbering nor content.

He strengthened the connection they shared, their hands intertwined, and with his free hand, he gently brushed away her tears. He held a silent wish, yearning to dispel the possibility of ever seeing her cry again.

Penny felt the warmth in the touch of his hand on her cheeks. Her heart raced as she leaned in a bit closer, her fingers lightly grazing his arm in an affectionate gesture. She felt the warmth of her feelings for Clauvère overwhelming her, and a contented sigh escaped her lips. Her other hand tightened perceptibly within his, mirroring how his grip had drawn in hers. Their fingers intertwined, creating a bond that seemed to ease the turmoil of the world around them. The admission to herself, prior to vocalizing her emotions, had been enough to throw her world off center. Now, sitting sedate next to Clauvère, things were different.

She realized that the harsh and cruel words Clauvère had used in instructing his man-at-arms on how to respond to Elizabeth had less of an impact on her than admitting her own feelings. In those few moments when she saw Clauvère in anger, she had also become acutely aware that this young boy was more than just that. He was Chevalier Clauvère Jean-Claude de La Pointierre, a mulatto from Martinique with French and Caribbean heritage. Furthermore, he was on the precipice of manhood, not just in age, but in his evolving mentality, especially the capacity for cruelty towards those who wronged him.

Penny firmly believed that the man she held deep affections for deserved not only her care but recognition for who he was and who he aspired to become. She felt an undeniable need to stand by his side, helping him to evolve into the man he was destined to be.

Penny had never hesitated to openly showcase her friendship with Clauvère, defying societal norms that urged her to do otherwise. Now, she was resolute in her determination never to hold back any expression of her feelings for Clauvère, whether in the public eye or behind closed doors.

In a tender moment, Clauvère spoke softly, addressing Penny, "Ma belle, Penny Chanceuse." (My beautiful, Lucky Penny.)

Penny reciprocated with equal affection, responding, "Mon Seigneur, mon beau trèfle à quatre feuilles" (My Lord, my handsome four-leaf clover.)

They continued in this manner for a while longer, exchanging soft words in French, their connection deepening, while Elizabeth observed from the doorway of the drawing room. Soon, Elizabeth stepped away from the door frame and made her way to the kitchen.

As Elizabeth departed, Amelia seized the opportunity to slip into the drawing room and engage with the two of them.

"Penny," she began hesitantly.

Amelia's voice disrupted the intimate atmosphere between Penny and Clauvère. Both of them shifted their attention to Amelia and offered her a weary smile, the aftermath of the recent tension clearly taking its toll on them.

Penny reached out her hand to her sister, who, holding back tears, slowly settled down on the floor at her younger sister's feet. Her head found a comfortable place on Penny's lap, and Penny's fingers began to gently caress her scalp.

"What happened out there," Amelia eventually inquired, her voice bearing a mix of concern and curiosity.

Penny cast a hesitant glance at Clauvère and, with a simple nod from him granting his tacit approval, she recounted the verbal altercation that had unfolded in a language her sister couldn't comprehend. Penny translated the words that had nearly brought chaos into their home.

Amelia, taken aback by the revelation, sat up abruptly in shock. Her hand instinctively covered her open mouth as she gasped in astonishment.

Amelia's complexion drained of color as the full weight of Clauvère's determination to assert his right to be treated equally, regardless of his skin color or noble status, became apparent. She experienced a tumult of emotions, simultaneously proud of his resolve and fearful of the extent of his power and his willingness to wield it without hesitation.

A fleeting image flitted through her mind: Aunt Elizabeth lying in a pool of her own blood in the mansion's entryway, a consequence of insulting a nobleman who happened to be of African descent. An involuntary shiver coursed through her. It was not because of the gruesome scene she had imagined but because the *man* capable of issuing such a command and committing such an act was none other than the gentle, caring boy who sat serenely beside her sister. He was dangerously close.

"I'm so sorry you had to endure that, Clauvère," her apology rang with heartfelt sincerity. Amelia continued, her voice laced with empathy, "It's unforgivable what some people are capable of, especially when they target you."

Amelia was jolted by the sound of a throat clearing. She swiveled her gaze towards the door, where her aunt, Elizabeth, had appeared. A surge of concern washed over her as she pondered what Elizabeth might think of her remark. Amelia had no doubt that the latter portion of her statement had been overheard.

In the drawing room, as Amelia, Clauvère and Penny chatted about the recent events that had just occurred, their friendship had shown signs of blossoming like the petals outside, Elizabeth swept into the room with an air of disapproval. Her expression was as frosty as the porcelain tea set she carried.

Elizabeth observed Clauvère and Penny's nearness with a scrutinizing gaze. They seemed practically intertwined, she mused, their closeness undeniable. Her disapproval of their strong bond was clear, as she regarded it as improper.

"Penelope," she scolded, her voice oozing with disapproval, "It is entirely unsuitable for a young lady to display such familiarity with a gentleman." Under her breath, and out of earshot, she added, "especially a young man of color."

She was determined to discourage their friendship. She decided to attempt to persuade George, when he got home later, to intervene. The hope was that he would put a stop to their interactions.

Penny's eyes widened, and Clauvère shifted uneasily in their shared seat on the settee. They hadn't caught the whispered remark, but its bitterness had nevertheless tainted the room's atmosphere. Tension hung heavy in the air as Elizabeth continued to scrutinize Penny.

"Je m'appelle Penny, pas Penelope," Penny retorted.

Elizabeth's eyes widened with curiosity. She hadn't comprehended a word of Penny's reply. She blinked as it dawned on her that Penny had responded in French.

"What did you say, young lady? Repeat that in English," Elizabeth demanded.

In response, Penny released Clauvère's hand, crossed her arms, closed her eyes, and turned her face away from her aunt.

Clauvère shifted his posture, crossing his legs and folding his arms. He regarded Elizabeth with a hint of disdain. "She said that her name is Penny, not Penelope."

"Well, I've never..." Elizabeth began, her voice trailing off into silence. She scanned the room for support, only to realize she stood alone, as the prevailing sentiment among those present, fueled by the earlier exchange in the mansion's entryway, left her isolated.

Elizabeth placed the tea set down on the coffee table and continued to speak as if the incident had never occurred. "Our family has a long-standing tradition of upholding the values and propriety that befit our station. You must not forget your responsibilities, child."

Penelope's gaze dropped to her lap, her cheeks flushing with a mixture of embarrassment and frustration. On the other hand, Clauvère couldn't help but bristle at the insinuation that his friendship with Penny was somehow improper.

Observing how Penny reacted to Elizabeth's spiteful words, Clauvère grew increasingly displeased. Though he felt an urge to lash out, he refrained from doing so and instead chose to wield the power of his words.

"I assure you, Mrs. Salisbury," Clauvère spoke in a measured and deliberately sarcastic tone as he enunciated her name, "our relationship is one based on mutual respect and nothing more." He extended his hand, taking Penny's, which caught her by surprise and made her blush profusely.

The falsehood in Clauvère's words was betrayed by his action of clasping Penny's hand in his own. He wore a satisfied smile as he noted the crestfallen expression on Elizabeth's face.

Elizabeth scowled. Her disapproving eyes met Clauvère's, and in that brief moment, an unspoken battle of wills raged.

Several hours passed as Penny and Clauvère deepened their connection through hushed conversations, all while under the watchful gaze of Elizabeth. In the room heavy with tension, Amelia began to feel like an outsider, mostly ignored by the two as they were engrossed in their own world.

As the time for Clauvère's departure approached, he made the announcement to the women present. Elizabeth, with an air of formality, escorted the young black noble to the mansion's entrance and bid him a brief and perfunctory farewell. Clauvère, in response, turned to her and offered a bitter smile.

"Remember your place as a commoner," he said flatly, with no emotion. There was not even a condescending tone in his words. His words cut deep. Clauvère had astutely perceived Elizabeth's longing for the prestige that came with socializing with nobility from the very beginning. He strategically wielded his words to inflict maximum damage on her.

The words cut deep. Clauvère had long since recognized Elizabeth's hunger for proximity to nobility, her fixation on status as a means of self-elevation. He wielded that knowledge deliberately now, delivering the remark without heat or contempt — not to provoke her, but to leave her defenseless against it.

In a world that so often sought to diminish him, the irony was unmistakable: it was he, a young Black nobleman, who reminded her where she stood.

Clauvère held little regard for rigid social classes, whether they involved royalty, nobility, the landed gentry, or commoners. His parents had instilled in him the belief that one's worth should be determined by their character, not their titles or the color of their skin. This perspective allowed him to see beyond the social boundaries that constrained so many.

When Clauvère noticed the depth of Elizabeth's yearning to elevate her social standing, it provided him with the perfect leverage to confront her. He understood that as long as he prodded at this particular vulnerability of hers, he could effectively counter any attempts she might make to undermine him. Their dynamic hinged on this unspoken understanding, with Clauvère subtly challenging her societal aspirations and prejudices.

Clauvère recognized that he could continually unsettle her by emphasizing a simple but powerful truth: he was a noble, and she was not. Despite his African Caribbean heritage, in the context of her own beliefs about nobility, this fact automatically positioned him higher in the hierarchy, irrespective of her being of white ethnicity. This dynamic allowed Clauvère to assert his authority while subtly challenging her entrenched views on social status and race.

Amelia, concealed in the shadows, watched in silence as Clauvère made his departure. The parting words he uttered reverberated through her, sending an unexpected chill down her spine. It was as though a curtain had been drawn back, revealing a hidden facet of Clauvère's character, one far more intricate and profound than the image he had previously projected. In that fleeting moment, she grappled with a startling revelation: the boy she thought she knew so well was, in truth, a person of remarkable complexity, capable of wielding an unsettling and unexpected aura of menace.

The stark contrast between the Clauvère she had perceived and the one she now witnessed left her with a sense of both disquiet and curiosity, prompting her to reconsider her understanding of this enigmatic young nobleman. 'Who is the real Clauvère?' she pondered, her thoughts in disarray. 'Am I looking at 'Chevalier Clauvère' or 'Clauvère' or are they the same person?

George Hartford returned to his chaotic household that evening, only to find Elizabeth, his sister-in-law, urgently demanding his attention. She was insistent on discussing pressing matters that couldn't wait. George, feeling the need for a moment of relaxation, assured her that he'd make time to listen but left the timing unspecified.

Seeking refuge in his study, George adamantly refused to meet with anyone else. In secret, he arranged for one of his trusted staff members, who happened to possess a working knowledge of French due to their English and French heritage, to brief him on the day's events. This staff member relayed the happenings in the grand hall of the estate.

Once George learned what had occurred, he grappled with a mix of shock and relief. It dawned on him that he had forgotten to inform his sister-in-law about Chevalier Clauvère's visit. He also chastised himself for not adequately preparing Elizabeth for the complexities of the de La Pointierre family dynamics

Reflecting on the matter, he scolded himself, muttering, "Why should I have made such a fuss of that when I have never cared about Minuette and her son Clauvère's mixed heritage for two years? It appears that Elizabeth learned her place from Chevalier Clauvère today due to her inclinations." He deliberately thought of Clauvère using his noble title due to his understanding of how Elizabeth worshiped the thought of the nobility and had an inflated infatuation with all things noble.

George made a deliberate choice to first connect with his daughters Amelia and Penelope before addressing their challenging aunt. He reassured himself with the commitment to follow up their conversation with another visit, aiming to cleanse the palate, so to speak, from his interactions with Elizabeth.

About an hour later, George extended an invitation to Elizabeth, requesting her presence in his study to discuss her concerns. His choice of location was calculated, emphasizing their distinct roles in the household and family. He positioned himself behind an elaborate desk in a plush chair, while offering a simple wooden and leather seat, the comfort of which was questionable, for Elizabeth to occupy on the other side of the desk.

Drawing from his experiences as a merchant, George employed a few tricks to influence the duration of their conversation. The chair designated for Elizabeth lacked armrests and sat conspicuously isolated in front of the desk. A wry smile crossed his face as he realized that even he would find that seat uncomfortable for extended conversations, considering how it was arranged in the room.

Indeed, Elizabeth appeared uncomfortable, yet it was evident that her discomfort did not stem from the seating arrangement.

In the days following her arrival, Elizabeth's presence had cast a formidable shadow over the Hartford estate, transforming the once carefree atmosphere into one charged with restraint. That culminated into the fiasco that had occurred in his home today.

Elizabeth launched into her discourse with unwavering determination, vehemently expressing her disapproval of the budding friendship between Clauvère and Penelope. She carried the heavy burden of concern, believing that the young woman grappled with a profound internal conflict, attempting to reconcile her family's traditional values with her heartfelt desires to be away from the influence of Clauvère, at least in Elizabeth's estimation.

George's brow creased. A single idea appeared. '*Why would Elizabeth think...*'

He leaned back in his chair.

'*Penny? Away from Clauvère?*' George thought. '*I think not.*'

But his mouth remained closed.

Silence ruled instead.

And thought.

George couldn't help but reflect on how misguided Elizabeth's perspective was and how far removed from reality it seemed. He wondered if she had genuinely taken the time to understand her nieces before making such overtly misguided comments about them. Her presumptions about the girls' thoughts and beliefs struck him as nothing short of outrageous.

“That young black noble stormed into the house and nearly frightened poor Amelia to death. He audaciously took Penelope’s hand and professed his love for her,” Elizabeth exclaimed with enthusiasm.

Her eyes darted back and forth, and she gesticulated animatedly as she recounted the scene.

George listened patiently and discerned that the only veracious aspect of her account, or at least the one he could reasonably believe, was Clauvère’s declaration of love for Penny. He wasn’t a fool, nor was he oblivious; he recognized the unmistakable signs of love when he saw them. Clauvère mirrored his own youthful infatuation when he courted his late wife.

It was just like his daughter and the young man, who he had no doubt, could soon become his son in law, to have engaged in outrageous behavior. In truth, he had been anticipating this development all along, given their deepening connection.

While the notion of his beloved daughter finding love with someone so remarkably impressive pleased George, it was marred by his deep concerns for their future. He was uncertain how their relationship would thrive in the American colonies, and he had received assurances that it wouldn’t.

“Are you paying attention?” Elizabeth’s voice pierced the air, and her hands dropped into her lap.

George pinched the bridge of his nose and closed his eyes. “I’m listening. Please continue.”

Elizabeth launched into a tirade about Clauvère’s father Louis — whom she had yet to meet personally, and his decisions and their wisdom. “I can’t believe Clauvère’s father married that negress woman of African descent,” she commented.

George let out an exasperated sigh. “Her name is Minuette. She’s of both French and Caribbean heritage. Her Caribbean lineage doesn’t even comprise entirely of African ancestry. So how can you refer to her as a ‘negress,’ Elizabeth?”

Elizabeth stood with her hands on her hips, her cheeks flushed with disbelief that her brother-in-law seemed to be aligning himself with those individuals, referring to the people of African descent and their relationship with that white Frenchman. “You ought to reconsider your stance, George.

I believe you should sever your ties with that Louis de La Pointierre and his...wife," she added with a tone of repulsion.

She couldn't bring herself to mention Clauvère, their son, as the very thought of him triggered a resurgence of the profound sense of insignificance she had felt when he departed the Hartford house earlier in the day, along with his parting words.

Those words reverberated, unwelcome and unerring, in her mind, compounding her feelings of smallness and insignificance. "Remember your place as a commoner." The way he gazed at her, not from above but directly into her eyes, made her feel less significant than even mouse droppings.

It was the very fact that he didn't deem her significant enough to cast even a condescending glance her way, as if doing so would bestow upon her some semblance of importance. Though a part of her longed to shed tears, she staunchly resisted, refusing to yield to that young man and his hurtful words.

Elizabeth wrestled with great effort to disentangle herself from these thoughts. The principal reason for her difficulty in extricating her mind from Clauvère's memory was the indelible impression he had left on her soul. While her social beliefs repelled the idea of associating with people of color, she couldn't deny being captivated by the sheer force and presence Clauvère exuded in those final moments before his departure.

Elizabeth sat back down. "You cannot rely on that man as a business partner!" Elizabeth declared emphatically.

Unabashed, George inquired, "That man's name is Louis so stop calling him in that manner. And why do you believe that?" He genuinely sought her reasoning.

Elizabeth regarded George as though he should already understand. "You can't trust Louis's decision-making skills. I mean, just consider his choice of a spouse, for goodness' sake!"

George's hand crashed down onto the surface of his imposing desk. At 36 years old, he remained a robust man, and the desk, constructed from solid, dense wood, issued a loud protest in response to the forceful slap, trembling as it did so. He paused, taking several deep breaths.

"Elizabeth, be mindful of your position. Chevalier Louis Jean-Baptiste de La Pointierre is a man, a noble, my business partner, and my friend," George murmured, his tone unwavering but gentle. "I believe our conversation has come to an end. You may take your leave now."

George's softly spoken words were mirrored as an echo in her mind, *Woman, recognize your place. He is a man, a nobleman, and he is my friend.*

Elizabeth wore a look of surprise at her abrupt dismissal, poised to voice a protest. However, when her gaze met George's unfiltered stare, she grasped that the conversation had extended as far as he was willing to tolerate.

Elizabeth's mouth snapped shut, and she rose slowly, offering George a small, respectful bow. "You're right. I'm sorry; I'll retire for the evening," she replied calmly.

As she made her exit, George decided it was time to deliver a piece of news he'd intended to convey differently but felt compelled to share now. He resolved to avoid further conversation with her until necessary. "We have an invitation to dine at the de La Pointierre estate in three days. Make sure you're prepared because you'll be attending as well."

Elizabeth had been halfway to the door when George relayed the news. She paused, and her shoulders visibly slumped as she drew into herself, arms wrapped tightly around her waist. George regarded her with a sense of compassion.

In a soft, defeated tone, Elizabeth asked, "Why are we going to dine with them?" Her voice reflected the unexpected turn the conversation had taken.

George explained, "Louis and I discussed it and concluded that our families haven't had much contact lately. They miss my daughters and are eager to reconnect with them."

Without turning back to face him, Elizabeth nodded slowly and exited his study with a dignified demeanor. "I'll ensure they're prepared for the dinner, then."

George remained oblivious to the tears that streamed down Elizabeth's cheeks, as her back was turned to him, and she ultimately let them flow freely, unable to keep them at bay any longer.

"One last thing before you leave, Elizabeth," George called out. "You need to watch what you say and to whom you say it. Do you know what Chevalier Clauvère told his man when he called him into the house?"

George's query was met with silence so he continued. "He told him that if you insulted him one more time, to slit your throat with his sword. Thibault would have done it in a second if you had persisted."

George noted the visible shiver that flowed through her body. She moved forward once more towards the door. With a gentle touch, she closed the door behind her as she left the room.

George let out a deep breath, expelling the tension from his body. After a moment of gathering himself, he resolved to shift his focus, deciding it was time for the second private moment of the evening he had initially promised himself with his daughters earlier in the evening.

The grand dining room of the de La Pointierre household was a scene of exquisite opulence, with polished mahogany furniture and shimmering candlelight. As the guests gathered for a family dinner, Clauvère seized the opportunity to assert his presence with Elizabeth.

"Mrs. Salisbury," he said in a gentle tone that brooked no argument, "please, have a seat next to me."

His request was delivered with an air of assumed authority that caused a few raised eyebrows around the table at the unexpected courtesy being extended to Elizabeth.

Elizabeth found herself ill at ease with Clauvère's request. She couldn't help but sense the incongruity between her age and her commoner status, which should have, by societal norms, placed her far from the heir of the house. Yet, his unyielding insistence possessed an audacious and disquieting quality that compelled her reluctant compliance, almost without conscious thought.

As soon as she settled in beside him, Clauvère swiftly redirected his attention elsewhere, immersing himself in the lively discourse unfolding between George and his father, Louis. The topics at hand revolved around recent city happenings. With dedication, he acted as the bridge, quietly relayed the livelier turns of conversation to his mother, who sat on his opposite flank. Minuette understood much of what was said, but the rapid English idioms—layered with humor and politics—often blurred together. When meaning slipped past her, she would tilt her head ever so slightly, and Clauvère, sensing it, supplied the thread she'd missed.

Clauvère couldn't help but notice the occasional puzzled glances from Penny. It was clear that she had anticipated sitting beside him and was taken aback by the presence of her aunt, whom she didn't hold in high regard. The question lingering in Penny's mind was why Clauvère had made this decision, given the tumultuous first encounter between the two of them.

However, Penny wasn't the only one bewildered. Every so often, George would cast his gaze their way, clearly perplexed by the unfolding dynamics. His wariness stemmed from his knowledge of Elizabeth's prejudiced views towards people of color.

During the dinner, Clauvère's interaction with Elizabeth remained minimal, limited to a few perfunctory nods and brief exchanges. Penelope, positioned across from them, couldn't help but watch Clauvère. Her heart ached at the realization that he hadn't afforded her the opportunity to sit closer to him.

As the first course arrived, Clauvère took charge. He deftly served Elizabeth, placing precisely measured portions on her plate without even looking at her. His hands moved with confidence and control. To Elizabeth, it felt as though he was curtailing her independence and decisions, a subtle but powerful reminder of their unequal positions in this society.

The conversation flowed around them, but Clauvère seemed to exist in a world of his own, his attention fixed on everyone and everything but Elizabeth. Even when her plate was cleared for the next course, he made no effort to engage with her preferences or desires, leaving her at the mercy of his choices.

Whenever Elizabeth was offered the courtesy of questions aimed at involving her in the conversation, her responses were either preempted by Clauvère's prompt responses on her behalf or she would lapse into silence when met with his direct, vacant gaze, as if awaiting her reply.

This conspicuous display of dominance went against the prevailing norms of the era, where young men were expected to treat women with deference, especially in the presence of their families. It was a stark departure from the behavior expected within both households, as social status didn't typically dictate interactions between their members. However, Elizabeth, having recently joined the Hartford household after immigrating from England, remained unaware of these particular dynamics.

Amelia observed the scene from the corner of the room, her young eyes wide with surprise and curiosity. She had known Clauvère as the cheerful, brave boy she admired. What she saw now was a different side, a Clauvère who wielded power and influence in ways she had never expected. Her thoughts danced in disarray, pondering who the real Clauvère might be — 'Chevalier Clauvère' or the one she thought she knew.

Around the table, unspoken tension simmered, intensifying Elizabeth's unease as she navigated the precarious social minefield. With each passing moment, her sense of disquiet grew. She couldn't help but wonder whether Clauvère's behavior was a calculated act of cruelty or if it stemmed from a genuine desire to find common ground with her, given the significant age difference, his noble status, and societal expectations.

Louis, perceptive to the situation, eventually felt compelled to address it. "Elizabeth, is my son's behavior bothering you in any way?"

Elizabeth paused, contemplating whether to voice her opinion. The traditional norms of how she should behave in the presence of nobility seemed to have been disregarded. Her confusion deepened as she observed the interactions between her brother-in-law George, her nieces Amelia and Penelope, and the de La Pointierre family.

She prepared to respond, but her words caught in her throat as she noticed Clauvère's intense and unsettling gaze fixed upon her once more. Frustrated, she glanced behind her, where Thibault stood against the wall just over Clauvère's shoulder. Her gaze then drifted down to the partially eaten food on her plate, and her hands, clasped demurely in her lap.

In a small voice, she finally managed to speak, shaking her head gently. "No," she replied, "Your son is being the perfect host."

Minuette, though she grasped enough of the exchange to sense discomfort, waited for her son to bridge the courtesy aloud. She nudged her son with an elbow, signaling him to pay attention and provide an interpretation of what had just transpired. As Clauvère began to speak, Minuette unexpectedly rose from her seat and circled around her son to stand behind Elizabeth.

Minuette extended a gentle hand to Elizabeth's shoulder, offering a warm smile as she suggested, "Allons nous rafraîchir" (Let's go freshen up.) she said then paused. "Let's go... parlor."

Elizabeth turned her gaze toward Minuette, a hint of confusion in her eyes. Reluctantly, she looked to Clauvère, silently beseeching him for an explanation. It was an uncomfortable situation, having to rely on Clauvère even for a simple translation. She could have just as easily asked Louis or her niece Penelope to help, but her thoughts were clouded by the evening's peculiar dynamics.

Throughout the dinner, Clauvère had taken control of her serving portions, making decisions without her input and effectively eroding her agency and autonomy. It was a stark demonstration of his power over her, underscoring the imbalance in their relationship. He had dominated her to the point where she felt on the verge of tears, believing she had no choice but to depend on him.

Though Minuette had long understood English, she still preferred to let others speak it. To her, words carried more than meaning—they carried manner, and she would rather remain silent than risk inelegance.

Minuette nudged her son once more and cast a disapproving frown in his direction. In response, Clauvère finally relayed, "My maman wants to know if you'd like to go and freshen up, Mrs. Salisbury."

Elizabeth's relief was palpable, almost verging on giddiness, as she realized she had been granted a reprieve from Clauvère's overwhelming attentiveness. She nodded enthusiastically but, in her eagerness, stumbled slightly as she rose from her chair.

As Elizabeth got up, all the men at the table promptly stood in a show of courtesy. However, when Minuette had done the same earlier, their attempt to extend the same courtesy was thwarted, as she had moved too swiftly for them to react.

With the departure of the two ladies, dinner conversation, or rather its semblance, came to an abrupt halt. It was as if an unspoken command had spread through the room. Both Amelia and Penny, who had fallen into silence earlier during the dinner after witnessing Clauvère's actions, now placed their forks in their plates and folded their hands in their laps, casting their eyes downward. They seemed fearful of drawing any attention to themselves. Meanwhile, George reclined in his chair, his expression marred by a scowl directed at Clauvère.

Even the unease of the servants stationed around the room was palpable, mirroring the awkwardness of the situation. These individuals, though in a subordinate position, were not oblivious to the unfolding dynamics. It wasn't their place to interject into the events occurring among those they served, but it was abundantly clear that they were all acutely aware of Clauvère's overbearing behavior.

It was Louis who took the initiative in the impending confrontation. He drew a deep breath and leaned in from his seat at the head of the table, directing his words to his son in French. He chose this language as he felt a sense of embarrassment discussing what he needed to address in the presence of his friend.

Louis was fully aware of Penelope's fluent understanding of French by this point, a fact he couldn't ignore but he pressed on regardless. "Qu'est-ce que ça veut dire, mon fils?" (What is the meaning of this, son?) he inquired, not concealing his disapproval.

Clauvère met his father's gaze with candor, making no attempt to evade the question or feign innocence. He responded, "Que veux-tu dire, père?" (What do you mean, father?) in a straightforward manner.

Louis struggled to contain his anger, though it remained just below the surface. "À quoi pensais-tu en faisant ça à cette femme à ma table?" (What were you thinking of, doing that to that woman at my dinner table?) he hissed, addressing his son.

Clauvère responded with flat detachment, addressing his father in English. "I was entertaining our guest, but if you think I was overattentive, then I guess my job as a host is done."

Rising from his seat, Clauvère's attendant, Thibault, assumed a posture that clearly indicated his unwavering attention to his young lord. This change did not escape Louis's notice, and he was taken aback by how Thibault now seemed to serve his son instead of him.

Clauvère continued, his tone unchanged. "If there is nothing else, Father, I think I will retire for the evening." He turned his attention to George and Amelia, offering a polite nod. "It was a pleasure dining with you. If you'll excuse me."

Penelope's eyes shot up in surprise. She locked onto Clauvère, realizing he hadn't addressed her yet. To her amazement, she saw him extending his hand toward her.

"Ma belle, Penny Chanceuse," (My beautiful, Lucky Penny.) Clauvère began in a soft tone, "Would you care to join me for a walk through the garden?"

Penelope's gaze drifted around the table at the remaining faces. She understood that she faced a choice, one that could carry potential repercussions if she decided to leave with Clauvère. Dabbing the corners of her mouth with her kerchief, she finished and found that Thibault had silently moved to her side of the table. He stood behind her, ready to pull out her chair should she decide to stand.

"Oui, Mon Seigneur. Mon Clauvère à quatre feuilles," (Yes, My Lord. My four leaf Clauvère.) Penny replied gently and softly.

Upon her standing, her father George and Louis instinctively rose out of habit. No words were spoken as Clauvère rounded the table and took Penelope by the hand, leading her away.

George glanced over at Louis and commented, "He is going to be a remarkable man when he gets older."

George did not say whether that realization comforted him—or unsettled him.

Louis sighed, expressing his realization. "I'm afraid that he's already a remarkable man."

For good or worse, both men agreed on that.

ELIZABETH SALISBURY

6

The de La Pointierre family and their guests reconvened in the drawing room. The elegant drawing room of Clauvère's family home was adorned with intricate furnishings, exuding an air of sophistication. Mr. and Mrs. de La Pointierre were seated on a plush couch, engaged in a conversation with Penelope's father George. The atmosphere was one of congeniality, despite the incident at the dinner table, their earlier encounter with Clauvère fresh in their minds. Both the boy in question, and Penelope were not in attendance.

Even so, they decided to speak on a different topic than the events at dinner.

Louis cleared his throat and addressed George. "George, there have been recent developments in the West Indies concerning the sugar imports and it's given rise to concerns on both sides of the ocean."

George, his posture exuding a mix of attentiveness and understanding, nodded in agreement. "Indeed, Louis. The disruption in the trade route due to the ongoing conflicts and political tensions is troubling."

Minuette had been given a running translation of the conversation by Louis. She interjected gently. "It's a dire situation, and one that requires careful consideration. The plight of the laborers in the sugar plantations is heart-wrenching. The recent weather in the Caribbean is threatening this year's crops and that will only further strain the political tensions already disrupting trade."

George, reflecting empathy in his voice, responded, "These matters remind us of the interconnectedness of our world. Our thoughts extend to those who are caught in the midst of these trials."

Elizabeth, standing slightly off to the side, observed the others with a sense of respect for their ability to discuss such matters with poise. Amelia, by her side, exchanged a knowing glance with her. While not directly involved in the discussions, they understood the importance of what was happening in the Caribbean and that it would likely affect their lives as well.

Louis leaned forward, his voice carrying a note of resolve. "George, I believe it's crucial that we consider potential avenues for aid and cooperation. Our collective efforts could potentially alleviate the suffering on both sides of the sea."

George nodded appreciatively. "Louis, you speak wisely. Our shared concern for the well-being of our fellow humans can serve as a driving force for positive change. Perhaps there are ways in which our communities can come together to provide support."

As the conversation continued, Elizabeth understood that in a time when the world was grappling with hardships and divisions, the exchange between these families showcased the power of unity and the potential to make a difference, even in matters that spanned continents and oceans. These thoughts were in conflict with the inner turmoil she was going through after her experience with Clauvère at the de La Pointierre dinner table.

The conversation did eventually drift in that direction, as Elizabeth had expected. Clauvère's actions had had a significant impact on all of them. Each had their unique perspective on the young noble's actions during the dinner, and they couldn't help but discuss their interpretations of Clauvère's behavior.

As they settled back into their seats, it was George who spoke first, addressing the others with a thoughtful expression. "I have to say, I found Clauvère's boldness quite admirable. He doesn't conform to the expectations of his station or the norms of the time. In my opinion, we should accept people for who they are rather than judging them solely on their social status."

Amelia, the youngest in the room, looked puzzled. "But father, he was so different tonight. I've always known him as a cheerful boy. What happened to him?"

George, not entirely aware of the nuances at play, replied, "Well, Amelia, people change as they grow. Perhaps he's showing a different side of himself. It's not necessarily a bad thing."

Minuette chimed in, her voice soft but filled with understanding. Louis relating her words for everyone. "I believe I know what you mean, George. Clauvère has certainly come into his own. We've seen him evolve into a young man who doesn't conform to societal norms, but it's all a part of his growth."

Louis nodded in agreement, adding, "Indeed, my dear. It's alarming as well. I've watched him embrace his character and charisma, which I believe has become a positive aspect of his development." Louis looked over at Elizabeth as he continued to speak. He drew her attention as his words continued to unfold. "Tonight, he seemed to be more aggressive than I've ever seen him. For that, I apologize, Elizabeth."

Elizabeth, feeling ever demure from the treatment she had received from Clauvère earlier in the evening, just nodded and curtsied. "It is alright, My Lord. He was being a grateful host." Internally, Elizabeth shivered at the thought of how the young man had controlled her without even a single threat but solely through his charismatic manner.

As the family continued to converse, Elizabeth maintained a thoughtful silence. She did not know when it had become easier to measure herself against Minuette than to revisit the memory of Clauvère's gaze. One had demanded something of her. The other had not. Her feelings toward Clauvère were more complex and conflicted. She couldn't deny the captivating force of his presence but also felt repelled by his dominance. Her prejudices clashed with her fascination, leaving her caught in a web of emotions she wasn't quite ready to unravel.

Amelia could see some of the distress that her aunt was under. She reached out her hand, tentatively, afraid of being rejected for offering solace. Elizabeth looked down at the hand in surprise as it touched her fingertips. She looked into Amelia's eyes and gave a waning smile before she deliberately took Amelia's hand into her own and clasped it tightly. The simple gesture offering Elizabeth some fragment of stability for her emotions.

The conversation continued, with each person in the room revealing a different facet of Clauvère's character as perceived through their unique lenses. The dynamics within the de La Pointierre family and their guests had shifted, and this newfound understanding of Clauvère would influence their interactions in the days to come.

Beneath the moon's soft glow, Clauvère and Penny walked hand in hand, their silhouettes etched against the canvas of a starlit night. The crisp evening air whispered secrets of the world, and the fragrant garden embraced them in its tranquility. They had left behind the echoes of a fraught dinner table, seeking refuge beneath the celestial tapestry.

Penny glanced at Clauvère, her eyes reflecting the questions she'd held since the dinner's turbulent conclusion. Her voice was gentle as she spoke, addressing him with an unyielding reverence, “Mon Seigneur, pourquoi as-tu agi de cette façon?” (My Lord, why did you act that way?)

Clauvère turned his gaze toward the heavens, his expression pensive. The crickets serenaded their conversation, lending a sense of serenity to the night.

“Penny, I’ve come to realize that I can’t remain passive in my own life any longer,” he said quietly. “I can’t just exist and let the world dictate the terms I’m expected to live by. I refuse to let others decide that for me.”

He paused, his resolve settling in the still air—yet, he had not answered her question.

Penny lifted her face to meet his eyes, her admiration unmistakable. “Mon Seigneur, votre détermination est inspirante.” (My Lord, your determination is inspiring.)

Clauvère’s gaze drifted briefly to the moonlight as it caught in Penny’s pale hair. With a tender smile, he drew her closer and bent to press a soft kiss atop her head, the difference in their heights making the gesture effortless.

In that quiet closeness, he became aware of how easily the world tried to define things—people, relationships, meaning—by distinctions that never seemed to fit quite right. Standing there with Penny, he felt certain of only one simple truth between them, untouched by expectation or category: they were the same age, sharing the same moment, choosing for themselves what it would mean.

He and Penny differed in stature. They belonged to discrete genders. Countless other distinctions set them apart. However, amidst this mosaic of differences, the singular attribute where they found complete alignment was their age. Their birthdays fell within the same month, separated by only a few days, weaving a subtle yet profound connection into the fabric of their relationship.

His musings waned as he gently tugged at her hand, urging her to accompany him along the garden path. With an unspoken understanding, they continued their journey, resuming their intimate conversation where they had momentarily left off.

But as they continued walking, Penny’s inquisitiveness tugged at her. “Mais, Mon Seigneur Clauvère, qu’est-ce qu’il y avait ce soir ? La table du dîner?” (But, My Lord Clauvère, what was it about tonight? The dinner table?)

Clauvère glanced at her, a flicker of vulnerability in his eyes. "Tonight was a demonstration, Penny, of the person I'm becoming. It's about asserting my presence and challenging the norms. I've grown tired of being just another noble. Of being just another colored individual. I want to be myself."

Penny nodded, understanding the turmoil that had unfolded earlier. Yet, she couldn't help but ask, "Mon Seigneur, avez-vous un plan pour la suite?" (My Lord, do you have a plan for what comes next?)

Clauvère gave her a small, determined smile. "Penny, there's a fire within me. I've discovered my strength and who I want to be. I want that fire to burn brighter. That's my plan."

Clauvère extended his hand toward the star-studded sky, splaying his fingers wide. His gaze shifted between his own hand and the night sky. Observing that Penny hadn't yet discerned his purpose, he gently intertwined his fingers with hers, guiding her to mimic his gesture.

"The celestial expanse reveals countless possibilities," he began, his voice carrying a sense of wonder. "Even with both our hands stretched out, we can't encompass a tiny fraction of it." He paused for emphasis, clenching his free hand into a fist. "But if each star represents a potential," he continued, his tone resolute, "I'll seize one and make it mine, then share it with you."

Clauvère beamed at Penny, and their journey through the garden continued.

With each step, Penny continued addressing him as "Mon Seigneur." Clauvère finally turned to her, his eyes searching hers. "Penny, why do you insist on calling me that?"

Penny's answer was unwavering. "Because, My Lord Chevalier Clauvère, I know who you are. I know who you're meant to be. I'll always address you as My Lord because it's not just about your title; it's a reflection of the greatness you carry within you. You are my love, My Lord."

Clauvère found himself on the verge of tears, deeply moved by Penny's words. It wasn't the content of her message that struck him the most; it was the language she had chosen to convey it. This marked the very first time, over their two years of acquaintance, that she had addressed him in English and expressed herself in a complete paragraph.

A vivid memory surfaced in Clauvère's mind. He remembered that, after telling her mother, "I wish you weren't here," and subsequently losing her,

Penny had fallen silent, fearing that her words held the power to inflict harm. To protect against such fears, she had eventually resorted to speaking in French after meeting him and his mother, Minuette, who only spoke in French. Thus, Penny's recent utterance in English carried a profound significance for him, touching him in a way that nothing ever had or ever would. Clauvère knew that the sacrifice she had made in speaking English would forever endure in his heart.

Clauvère's excitement radiated as he gently but firmly held Penny by her shoulders. "What about you, Penny? How can I continue to support you?"

Penny gazed at Clauvère, a hint of confusion in her eyes. She pondered whether he was truly as oblivious as he appeared in that moment. "Don't you understand?"

Clauvère drew her nearer, seeking clarity. "Understand what?"

A gentle smile graced Penny's lips as she lovingly placed a hand on his cheek, her head tilting to the side. She let out a contented sigh. "You're already supporting me more than you realize. Do you not hear me speaking to you in English now?" Her other hand mirrored the affectionate gesture on his opposite cheek, and she rose on her tiptoes to plant a tender kiss on Clauvère's forehead.

Clauvère's heart swelled with the warmth of her understanding and support. Under the vast expanse of the starry night, he realized that their journey was not a solitary one, but one they'd walk together, hand in hand, as equals, under the shimmering tapestry of dreams yet to be woven.

A few days had passed. The lamps had been lit, though the sun had not yet fully surrendered the day. Their soft glow warmed the Hartford parlor just enough to chase away the evening chill without disturbing the hush that had settled over the room.

George sat in his chair near the window, papers forgotten on the side table beside him. Amelia occupied the sofa opposite, her hands folded neatly in her lap, posture composed but not rigid. She had been reading earlier, though the book now lay closed beside her, its place held by nothing at all.

George cleared his throat, not from discomfort, but from deliberation.

"Amelia," he said gently, "I wanted to ask you something. And I want you to answer honestly."

She looked up at once, attentive. "Of course, Father."

He hesitated just long enough to weigh his words. "This young man—Robert Waverly. He's been calling on you more frequently of late. I thought it best not to pretend I hadn't noticed."

A faint color rose in Amelia's cheeks. She lowered her eyes, lips curving into a small, embarrassed smile.

"I know I've given my permission for him to court you," George continued, his tone even, unpressured. "But that does not mean I expect anything of you. I only want to know—are you content with the idea of him pursuing you?"

Amelia's fingers tightened slightly where they rested together.

"I... I think he is kind," she said softly. "And earnest. I enjoy his company."

She paused, then added, quieter still, "I don't dislike the thought of it."

George nodded, satisfied with the honesty of the answer, and did not press her further.

That was when the sound of footsteps entered the parlor behind them.

Elizabeth stood just inside the doorway, having clearly overheard enough. She did not announce herself. She rarely did.

"How very... modern," she said, her voice smooth but cool. "To discuss such matters so openly."

Amelia stiffened. George did not turn at once.

Elizabeth stepped fully into the room. "A young lady's affections are not a topic for casual parlor conversation."

George turned then, expression calm. "We were speaking privately. As family."

Elizabeth smiled thinly. "And yet I hear the name Robert Waverly spoken as though he were already a fixture."

Her gaze shifted to Amelia. "Do you truly believe that boy is suitable?"

Amelia looked up, startled. "He is respectable, Aunt Elizabeth."

"Respectable," Elizabeth echoed, tasting the word. "Yes, I'm sure he is polite enough. But politeness does not build households."

George said nothing.

Elizabeth continued, warming to her point. "Does he possess land? A proper income? A future that does not depend on luck and borrowed optimism?"

Amelia hesitated—then straightened.

"I have my own earnings," she said.

The words landed softly. Decisively.

Elizabeth blinked. "Your—what?"

"My earnings," Amelia repeated, voice steady despite the color returning to her cheeks. "From tutoring."

Elizabeth's mouth tightened. "That is not a solution. A young woman does not earn. She is provided for."

George shifted in his chair.

Elizabeth pressed on, emboldened. "Money in a woman's hands is not independence—it is impropriety. A girl does not support herself. She prepares herself. For marriage. For obedience. For—"

"Enough."

The word cut cleanly through the room.

George stood.

The silence that followed was immediate and absolute.

He did not raise his voice when he spoke again. He did not need to.

"That is enough," he said, measured and final. "We will not argue in this house. And we will not reduce my daughter to a set of expectations you find comforting."

Elizabeth froze where she stood.

"This is not so dire a matter," George continued, "that I will permit strife under my roof."

Elizabeth inclined her head slowly. "As you wish."

Her voice had cooled, retreating into formality. "I believe I shall retire for the evening."

She turned and left the room without another word.

Amelia remained seated, blinking rapidly now, tears threatening but not yet falling. She did not look at her father.

George did not look at her either.

He turned instead toward the window, giving her the privacy of his back, allowing her dignity to remain intact.

The parlor returned to silence.

And there it stayed.

On the next day, the late-afternoon sun drifted lazily across the field behind the Hartford estate, warming the air beneath the wide oak tree where the children had gathered. Spring had coaxed them outdoors, and the rare stillness of the day made the world feel unusually gentle.

Clauvère had felt compelled to spend time with Penny but was uncomfortable with them spending time together alone. He coaxed Peter to join him to make it easier for himself. Peter, for his part, was delighted at the invitation. When he asked if Amelia would attend as well, he was informed that Amelia was playing the role of companion with his maman at the moment and at the de La Pointierre estate instead.

Upon Clauvère's arrival, Elizabeth's expression tightened, a small flicker of displeasure she masked almost immediately. She allowed his presence only because the families were close, because she had no wish to upset George, and because Peter was with them. And, with the kitchen staff able to observe the children from the window, propriety was—if barely—maintained.

Out in the yard, Clauvère tossed a leather ball upward, catching it with confident ease. Peter let out an appreciative whistle.

Penny crossed her arms, chin lifting just slightly. "Fais attention, Mon Seigneur. Tu vas finir par te faire mal." (Be careful, My Lord. You'll end up hurting yourself.)

Peter blinked, brow pinching. "She said... something about getting hurt, didn't she?"

Clauvère offered a small grin. "She said you should be careful. And she thinks I take too many risks."

Peter huffed. "She's right about the second part."

Clauvère laughed and sent the ball toward Penny. She caught it neatly, gave a quick, surprisingly elegant turn, and returned it with a perfect arc.

Peter stared. "Good Lord... Penny, how did you—"

"Depuis longtemps," (For a long time.) she replied, switching the ball to her other hand.

Peter glanced at Clauvère.

Clauvère translated with a shrug. "She says she always could."

Peter groaned. "Of course she did." Then under his breath, in the worst French he'd ever attempted, "Je... suis... impressionné?" (I... am... impressed?)

Penny blinked and tilted her head, brow knitting. "C'était une question? (Was that a question?)

Clauvère laughed softly. "Definitely."

Penny's expression softened; her laughter was soundless but unmistakable.

They fell into an easy rhythm after that—passing, dodging, stumbling through plays that were more enthusiasm than coordination. Penny spoke only in French, her voice light and sure; Peter kept up until he didn't, then tugged Clauvère's sleeve and muttered, "Alright, what did she say that time?"

Sometimes Clauvère translated. Sometimes he didn't—because Penny's teasing grin said enough.

Eventually they collapsed beneath the oak, chests rising with laughter rather than exhaustion. The quiet settled around them like a second shade.

Peter wiped sweat from his brow. "Penny... I may never keep up if you keep speaking only French."

Penny tipped her head, considering him. Then, slowly she said "Tu comprends plus qu'avant." (You understand more than before.)

Clauvère translated — but Peter had understood the shape of it even before he did.

He smiled back at her. "Maybe. With effort."

Clauvère reclined on his elbows, glancing between them. "It's because we're always together. You'll learn."

Penny nodded at that, her gaze drifting toward the sky above them. "Mon Seigneur, nous sommes bien ensemble." (My Lord, we are good together.) she said.

This time, neither boy needed the translation. However, Peter seemed to be confused. He glanced between Penny and Clauvère.

"Why does she call you that?"

Clauvère awkwardly became evasive. "It's... something she started doing recently. I'm not certain why."

Penny, blushing, avoided eye contact with either boy. "Je... préfère comme ça, Mon Seigneur." (I... prefer it this way, My Lord.)

Clauvère, having emboldened himself for her sake, turned and smiled, "Ma belle, Penny Chanceuse." (My beautiful lucky 'Penny'.)

Peter was want to speak but remained silent, recognizing a moment had passed without his inclusion but not feeling left out because of it.

Penny paused, then regarded Clauvère with a gentle smile. "J'ai quelque chose pour maman Minuette. Je veillerai à aller le chercher quand vous serez prêts à partir." (I have something for maman Minuette. I'll make sure to fetch it when you are ready to leave.)

Clauvère's brow furrowed. "Maman? What could it be?"

Penny laughed, the sound like tiny bells. "L'anniversaire de maman Minuette est demain, n'est-ce pas? (Maman Minuette's birthday is tomorrow, is it not?)

Clauvère groaned. "How could I forget," he said dramatically. "I am definitely an unfilial son."

Penny and Peter laughed.

The breeze moved softly through the oak branches, carrying the quiet certainty of her words. For that brief, unburdened moment, the three of them fit neatly into the world — a small, perfect piece of it.

That evening, as Clauvère and Peter enjoyed a carriage ride home, a rare moment of joy washed over him. The two friends engaged in playful banter, showcasing the camaraderie of young men growing together. Suddenly, a burst of inspiration struck Clauvère, prompting him to halt the carriage's journey through the city. Penny had just reminded him that his maman's birthday was soon. They were near the city now so he could use the time to find a gift.

He signaled the carriage driver, Thibault, a long-serving Frenchman—a chevalier in his own right, who had faithfully served the de La Pointierre family and managed the estate's stables despite being one of Louis' man-at-arms.

The driver peered down at Clauvère with a quizzical expression and inquired, "Chevalier Clauvère, es-tu sûr de vouloir t'arrêter ici maintenant dans la ville sans la compagnie de ton père?" (Chevalier Clauvère, are you sure about stopping in the city without your father's company?.)

Clauvère furrowed his brows, feeling a pang of uncertainty creep in. Thibault's words were unexpected, and he wondered why his friend would express concern at a time when his mind was entirely absorbed by the desire to find the perfect gift for his mother. Nevertheless, he appreciated the gesture.

Clauvère tried to dismiss the doubts, assuring the driver, "Thibault, mon ami, tout ira bien. Je reviendrai peu de temps après avoir acheté un cadeau pour ma mère." (Thibault, my friend, everything will be fine. I will return shortly after purchasing a gift for my mother..)

As Clauvère bid him farewell with a wave, Thibault watched them depart, his eyes betraying a subtle concern. Peter, who had diligently been learning French under the guidance of Clauvère's mother, Minuette, comprehended the exchange between the two, even though it unfolded in the French language.

Their regular lessons had significantly bolstered his command of the language, but there was a peculiar twist to their conversations when he, Penny, and Clauvère came together – they exclusively conversed in French. Penny, who had overcome her selective mutism, had now transitioned to speaking exclusively in French instead of English.

As Clauvère dismissed Thibault's concern, Peter couldn't help but wonder if his friend had caught the subtleties in Thibault's words. Concerned, he thought, "Clauvère is so determined, but does he truly grasp the unease that hangs in the air?"

Peter couldn't help but worry about the undertones in Thibault's words. He discerned that Thibault's concern for Clauvère was rooted in the young man's mixed racial heritage and how he might be perceived while shopping in the city. Peter suspected that Clauvère might have missed this subtlety and that Thibault's question was more about ensuring his safety than anything else.

As they strolled down the city street, Peter finally broached the topic. "Clauvère, do you understand why Thibault asked you that?" he inquired.

However, Clauvère remained unwavering in his determination. He was laser-focused on his mission – a visit to a confectionery he knew on this very street to purchase candies for his mother. Later, he planned to acquire some flowers to surprise her that evening upon his return.

"Thibault is overly concerned for my well-being. I don't need my father by my side to ensure my safety," Clauvère declared.

They reached the shop before Peter could voice his concerns further. An air of unease hung over him as he scanned his surroundings, vigilantly observing the people in the vicinity.

Upon Clauvère's entrance, the shop's proprietor wore a look of surprise on his face. His eyes betrayed his astonishment as he registered the presence of a young boy of African descent in his establishment. The shock was not just related to Clauvère's ethnicity but also to his attire.

"How can I assist you, boys?" the proprietor inquired, recovering from his initial surprise. He had expected Peter to be the spokesperson but was taken aback when Clauvère assumed the lead, both in his actions and his eloquence.

Clauvère, in a composed manner, replied, "I've come to select a gift for my mother. I'd like a few of the sweets you have here," he said, pointing to a particular confection that his mother favored, situated within the display case before him.

The proprietor's actions seemed sluggish as he hesitated, continuing to fixate on Clauvère. His surprise had left him momentarily at a loss for words, and the other customers present in the store had halted their perusal of the merchandise to observe the unusual and unfamiliar exchange unfolding before them. Hushed whispers reached Peter's ears, adding to his growing concern. Clauvère remained oblivious to these, his full attention trained on the proprietor and the completion of his transaction.

In an attempt to redirect Clauvère's attention, Peter stepped closer and gently touched Clauvère's arm. He opted to speak in French to shield their conversation from prying ears. "Je pense que nous devrions partir d'ici. Maintenant. Clauvère." (I think we should leave here. Now. Clauvère.)

Turning to face Peter, Clauvère appeared puzzled by his friend's urgency. Failing to comprehend Peter's unease, he replied, "We're almost done. One moment." Then, he turned back to the proprietor, inquiring, "How much?"

The proprietor swiftly named a price, and Clauvère retrieved his wallet. However, as the proprietor observed the amount and the assortment of bills within the wallet, his demeanor underwent a marked transformation.

"Where did you steal all of that money, boy?" the proprietor inquired, his tone laced with suspicion.

Clauvère cast a bewildered gaze upon the proprietor, and Peter's concerns deepened. Gradually, Clauvère's confusion transformed into anger. Clauvère's heart raced as indignation and anger welled up within him. The unjust accusation burned, but he was determined to stand his ground. "This money is mine. Why would I need to steal anything?" he retorted, his voice edged with indignation.

This response immediately shocked the onlookers, turning their whispers into astonished gasps. The proprietor, stepping out from behind the display counter, seized Clauvère by the arm. His voice took on a more demanding tone as he pressed, "Where did you get that money? Don't lie to me."

While watching Clauvère's interaction with the shop owner, Peter's heart ached for his friend. He knew that, as a young boy of African descent, Clauvère had to navigate a world that often misunderstood him. His own bond with Clauvère had deepened his understanding of these challenges. But to see these challenges right before his eyes though was something else entirely.

Peter quickly grabbed the proprietor's arm, the same one holding Clauvère, trying to make him let go. "Stop. He's not lying," he exclaimed, his voice filled with urgency.

"Let go of me," Clauvère thundered, his tone assertive and unyielding.

In response to Peter's interference, the proprietor tried to wrench his arm free, while simultaneously raising his other arm with the intention of striking Clauvère to extract the information he sought. But in the tense moment just before the blow could land, Clauvère's gaze caught the glint of a sword's tip emerging just below the man's jaw, directed squarely at his throat.

Thibault's voice, though broken in English, resonated through the space, delivering a stark warning. "Let the Chevalier Clauvère go, or you'll find a sword at your throat."

Clauvère turned to gaze at his unexpected savior. Clauvère's eyes met Thibault's with a silent 'thank you.' He could feel the warmth of appreciation wash over him. He promptly withdrew his arm from the loose grasp of the proprietor with a jerk.

"Est-ce que ça va, Chevalier Clauvère?" (Are you alright, Chevalier Clauvère?) Thibault inquired, concern lacing his tone.

Rubbing his arm with a scowl, Clauvère regarded the proprietor with a malevolent glare, his anger simmering beneath the surface. The impulse to urge Thibault to mete out justice hung in the air but remained unspoken. "Let's go," he eventually declared, his voice laced with an undertone of seething frustration.

The journey back home was shrouded awkward in silence. Clauvère's gaze remained fixed on the passing scenery beyond the carriage window, while Peter wrestled with a desire to console his friend, yet uncertainty about how to do so.

Peter remained silent, but he couldn't shake the worry that this incident might cast a shadow over their friendship. He was white and Clauvère, while of French nobility, was still considered to be black. He didn't want Clauvère to feel patronized, but he couldn't ignore the reality of the world they lived in. He was on the brink of saying something, anything, when Clauvère turned his eyes toward him.

"Please, don't ever mention what happened back there. I don't want others, especially my parents and Penny, to worry," Clauvère said gently. "And thank you for your support back there. You were a true friend," he added, offering a warm smile.

Peter returned the smile, though his internal turmoil ran deep. He burned with a desire to rectify the injustice his friend had endured.

As they reached their destination, Clauvère turned to Thibault and, in hushed tones, impressed upon him the importance of keeping the incident a secret. After some reluctance, Thibault agreed, with one condition: he would accompany Clauvère whenever the young boy ventured alone into the city from that point forward.

Clauvère hesitated for a moment, torn between wanting to assert his independence and realizing the value of Thibault's friendship. He weighed his desire for freedom against the fear of facing such prejudice alone. Remembering the turmoil of the recent ordeal, Clauvère nodded in agreement.

AMELIA HARTFORD

7

As the days unfolded, the fragile equilibrium of harmony within the Hartford household hung in the balance. George found himself wrestling with the intricate tapestry of relationships and tensions that had come to the forefront in light of Elizabeth's presence.

Elizabeth, on her part, remained a stern role model for her nieces, endeavoring to keep them engaged within the confines of their home and shielded from what she regarded as the negative influence of Clauvère, a young man of color. There were still moments when she couldn't shake the trepidation stemming from her memories of him, recalling how he had manipulated and held sway over her during that fateful dinner at the de La Pointierre residence.

The frequency of Clauvère's tutoring sessions had been curtailed to just twice a week, a decision largely instigated by Amelia. This change was warranted by Clauvère's commendable progress, but it was also a reaction to Elizabeth's insistence on attending the sessions at the de La Pointierre household, where her presence had begun to disrupt the flow of lessons.

Elizabeth persistently voiced her concerns to George regarding Clauvère's presence in the girls' lives, convinced that it would jeopardize their prospects for respectable and suitable marriages.

Louis, Clauvère's father, was not immune to Elizabeth's distant demeanor. His marriage to Minuette Notette only added fuel to Elizabeth's disapproval. Despite the intensity of her sentiments, she refrained from openly criticizing Louis, adhering to societal norms that upheld his autonomy in making life choices.

However, Elizabeth exhibited no such restraint when it came to Minuette. In the confines of the de La Pointierre household, she unapologetically snubbed Minuette, openly displaying her disdain for Louis's choice of a wife. The household of the de La Pointierres and the Hartfords quivered with tension as Elizabeth's traditional values clashed with the more liberal and progressive atmosphere embraced by each family.

That day, the gardens of the Hartford estate burst into full bloom, their colors exuberant under the caressing rays of the summer sun. Clauvère had paid a visit to the family, and after some hesitation, Elizabeth reluctantly permitted

Penelope to join him on a leisurely stroll through the garden. She trailed a respectable distance behind them, effectively assuming the role of a discreet chaperone for their rendezvous.

Penny's feelings for Clauvère had blossomed just like the flowers that surrounded them. Their friendship had grown deeper, their laughter and shared moments casting a gentle glow over their time together.

As they strolled down the garden path, Penny couldn't help but steal glances at Clauvère. His features were strong, his eyes filled with a mix of resilience and vulnerability. But she sensed a growing disheartenment in him, something that weighed on his soul.

"My Lord, Chevalier Clauvère, you seem troubled," she ventured, her concern evident in her voice.

Clauvère sighed, his gaze fixed on the distant horizon.

"Despite our freedom, we're met with prejudice and discrimination. It's disheartening," muttered Clauvère in a low tone, the words slipping out more as a thought than a confession.

Penny leaned closer—not quite to his ear, but to the hush of his voice. She hadn't fully heard what he said, only the weight carried in it.

Clauvère noticed her nearness, the concern gathering faintly along her brow. He turned to her with a small smile and slipped a hand to her waist, drawing her in just enough to anchor the moment.

"It's nothing, ma belle, chanceuse Penny," he said softly, before releasing her.

Penny's head dipped at once, her hand rising to cover the blush that warmed her cheeks. When she had steadied herself, she fell back into step beside him as they continued along the grass-lined path.

She gathered her thoughts, calming her heart, and cast him a sidelong glance as they walked. He hadn't lied to her — not truly. But neither had he spoken the truth.

Not in the way that mattered.

"Will you tell me?" she asked softly.

Clauvère slowed and turned to face her fully. "What would you have me tell you?" he asked. "That I hate what I've done recently to Elizabeth?" His gaze drifted briefly toward the house in the distance before returning to Penelope. "Or should I tell you—"

He stopped.

The pause stretched, heavier than the first. The words were there, pressing at the back of his throat—I love you—but the moment felt wrong. Too weighted. Too close to the bitterness still clinging to him from the city, from the shop, from the reminder of what the world insisted he be before it allowed him to be anything else.

His eyes dropped to the back of his hand. Dark against the pale afternoon light. A simple fact. An unavoidable one.

He turned away and began walking again, waiting until she fell into step beside him.

"I've had to deal with more ignorance than usual," he said at last, his voice carefully even. "Nothing you need trouble yourself with, ma belle—chanceuse Penny."

Penelope smiled.

False.

She couldn't decide whether she felt relieved that Clauvère was too caught in his own thoughts to see it—or quietly hurt that he was.

Still, she composed herself and walked on beside him, her heart aching in a way she didn't yet have words for. She had always known the world was unjust. What unsettled her now was realizing how often he had to carry that knowledge alone.

"We can begin with smaller steps," she said gently.

Clauvère glanced at her then, something warm and unspoken softening his expression. He brushed her hand lightly as they continued along the garden path, the words he had not spoken lingering between them—unvoiced, but very much alive.

"We can't change everything yet," she said quietly. "But we don't have to do nothing either. And later... maybe it won't feel so impossible."

Clauvère smiled at that and brushed his fingers against her hand. "I know," he said. "I believe that too. I just—" He hesitated, searching for the right words. "Right now, it feels like the world decides things for me before I ever get a chance. Like no matter what I do, every step is harder than it should be."

Their connection deepened further as they shared their dreams for a more equitable world, where the color of one's skin would not dictate their worth. Yet there remained an obstacle they had not been able to overcome.

That obstacle was Elizabeth. Whenever she was near, Penny's tongue tied in knots, and the words she had practiced so diligently seemed to abandon her. She had grown adept at shifting between languages with Clauvère, a skill she found both challenging and exhilarating, but in Elizabeth's presence it often failed her.

One afternoon, under Elizabeth's stern gaze, Penelope faltered, her French disappearing as if it had never existed. The lapse filled her with quiet frustration and a growing sense of resentment she struggled to name.

Clauvère, seated beside her, reached beneath the table and squeezed her hand. The gesture was small and unseen, but it steadied her, reminding her that the silence was not her own choosing.

In the quiet hours between breaks during tutoring sessions, Penelope and Clauvère found moments to speak freely, slipping past Elizabeth's notice. Their conversations moved between English and French, and with Clauvère's encouragement and Minuette's guidance, Penelope continued to make steady progress. Those private exchanges gave her a sense of resolve, as though each word learned carried her one step closer to the life she imagined.

These memories were heartwarming in their own way. But, in the gardens of the de La Pointierre estate, amidst the blossoming flowers and growing feelings, Penelope and Clauvère's connection was unbreakable, their determination to change the world resolute. The obstacles they faced only served to strengthen their resolve, and their love for each other bloomed like the most resilient of summer flowers.

Spring continued to bloom outside, its beauty in stark contrast to the internal conflict that now haunted the Hartford estate. Elizabeth's arrival had cast a shadow, but as the days passed, it remained to be seen whether the bonds of friendship could withstand the traditional values and societal pressures that threatened to tear them asunder.

Over the months living in the colonies, Minuette's ear had grown sharper. Once, English had been a language she understood but rarely used—a coarse melody she preferred not to play. Now, it reached her too easily. She caught the meaning behind the half-smiles, the soft insults wrapped in civility, the way her name lingered a fraction too long on certain tongues belonging to the white women in town.

But her discomfort was only one layer of the story. A deeper longing pulsed within her. It was a longing for her true home, the French West Indies, where the family's sugar plantation thrived. This desire to return became a constant presence, gnawing at her, pulling her heart toward a past she cherished.

To assimilate, she had begun to wear clothing reminiscent of the white women in Savannah instead of Martinique, but this choice only set her further apart, making her deeply uncomfortable in a world where she felt like an outsider.

During a particular social gathering, Minuette experienced a profound realization that she was out of her element. Elizabeth and Amelia had accompanied her to a tea gathering she had been explicitly invited to; an event attended by the city's high-society women. Minuette's presence was due to her noble status and her marriage to the son of a Count, of that she was certain.

The carriage rocked gently along the country lane, its wheels crunching over gravel while beams of sunlight filtered through the canopy overhead. Inside, Elizabeth sat opposite Minuette in an unspoken truce of proximity. Amelia lay asleep on Minuette's lap.

Dappled light flickered across Minuette's face, momentarily captivating Elizabeth with the quiet dignity of the woman before her—a woman whose background Elizabeth had scorned and whose son still left her uneasy.

Yet, in that fleeting instant, she couldn't deny Minuette's graceful composure or the ease with which she mothered Penelope when circumstances demanded. Here, with no onlookers to judge, Elizabeth felt oddly free—unwatched. The usual weight of others' expectations seemed less insistent.

Across from her, Minuette offered a polite, reserved smile, her hands folded in her lap. Elizabeth found it easier to bristle at Minuette than to recall Clauvère's gaze.

Clauvère was absent. Minuette was not.

Elizabeth's mind churned with questions she had never dared to voice aloud. Why do I feel so threatened by her? she nearly asked, but her courage wavered. Instead, her lips parted with a question both gentler and more revealing than anything she had said thus far.

"Do you ever find it difficult?" Elizabeth asked quietly, her gaze flicking to the passing countryside before settling back on Minuette. "Caring so dearly for a child who—who isn't... well, who isn't yours by birth?"

A flicker of uncertainty crossed her own face the moment the words left her mouth. She realized how blunt they might sound, but she needed to know.

Minuette studied Elizabeth for a moment, her dark eyes calm. She then glanced down at the young woman asleep in her lap. When she answered, her voice was soft, each word carefully chosen. "She... and Penny... she is mine in heart, Mrs. Salisbury. I see her and Penny... always... same as my own."

Elizabeth felt a sudden tightness in her chest. The carriage lurched over a small rut in the road, jostling them both. She cleared her throat, uncertain how to respond. Minuette's measured words—spoken in slightly halting English—carried a gentle conviction that Elizabeth found both humbling and disconcerting. She had half-expected to feel smug or vindicated, yet instead she felt... envious. Moved, even.

"I—see," she murmured, easing back into her seat. "That must be... kind of you."

Her own words felt hollow. A swirl of conflicting emotions rose inside her: envy, discomfort, and perhaps a whisper of admiration. Was Minuette truly so confident in her own worth that barbed remarks or implied slights could not wound her?

Silence settled between them. The thought had almost occurred to Elizabeth that she might apologize—if not for her question, then for something larger, something more insidious that festered beneath every forced civility. But the moment passed.

Minuette exhaled softly, turning her gaze toward the dappled sunlight beyond the window. By unspoken accord, their conversation waned. Only the rhythmic clatter of hooves and the carriage's low creaks filled the hush as they pressed on toward the luncheon. Neither woman spoke another word—yet each carried away the faint imprint of what might have been said if they had dared remain in that fragile, vulnerable space a moment longer.

Then a fleeting spark flared: Elizabeth caught a glimpse of tenderness in Minuette's eyes and felt an odd pang of sympathy. But a tide of disapproval rose swiftly in her mind—she reminded herself, again, that these people did not share her station. Under her breath, and more to herself than to Minuette, she murmured, "I've never really known a family like yours before. My parents taught me..."

Her voice trailed off. She felt the countless whispered rules that had shaped her upbringing. Yet she remembered how, when she saw Clauvère guiding Penny with such gentle care, she couldn't help but wonder if she was the one in the wrong. *What would my parents have said?* The uneasy thought lingered briefly, then echoed into silence. She turned her face away, choosing to stare out the window on the opposite side from Minuette's view.

And so the carriage rolled on in quietude, its occupants caught between unspoken questions and shared uncertainties—neither quite sure how to cross the tenuous bridge that had formed, however briefly, between them.

They arrived at a lavish mansion much later in the afternoon. Inside, the parlor was adorned with elegant furnishings. The attendees, a group of esteemed ladies, were seated at various tables scattered throughout the room.

As Minuette entered, a hush fell over the room, and curious gazes were fixed upon her, while the voices gradually dwindled into silence. Minuette, in an effort to maintain a pleasant demeanor, brushed off the scrutiny of their gazes. She was keenly aware of the tension in the room but refused to let it weigh her down.

Amelia's friend, Mary, hurried over to greet her. Mary spared a moment to appraise the company Amelia was with, acknowledging Elizabeth with a nod and a warm smile. Her exchange with Minuette, however, was noticeably more prolonged, as if she were taking extra time to study Minuette, mirroring the courtesy extended to Elizabeth.

After this moment of contemplation, Mary turned her attention back to Amelia, offering Minuette a somewhat subdued smile as she did so. Her demeanor seemed to brighten as her focus shifted back to her friend, Amelia.

"Amelia," she began, "How have you been?"

Amelia's smile radiated warmth as she clutched her small purse, her fingers tightening around it. Despite a subtle tremor in her hand, her cheerful expression remained intact.

"I'm fine," Amelia replied, her voice bright and chipper. She paused for a moment, briefly glancing over her shoulder at Elizabeth, who seemed preoccupied and not paying attention to her. Then, she redirected her focus to Mary. "Things have been... going well... at home."

Mary, not catching the subtle sarcasm in Amelia's response, returned her smile, thinking all was well.

"Where is the Countess? She was supposed to be escorted here by you," Mary inquired with enthusiasm. European nobility was a rarity in these parts, and the prospect of a Countess attending the tea party filled her and all the other ladies in the room with excitement.

Amelia gave her a quizzical look.

Mary misinterpreted Amelia's expression, believing that Amelia was unaware of whom she was inquiring about. Speaking in hushed tones, Mary added an air of secrecy to her words, "You know, the Countess Minuette de La Pointierre."

Amelia's eyes widened as she grasped Mary's misunderstanding. She corrected gently, "Madam Minuette Notette de La Pointierre isn't a Countess; her father in law holds that title."

"Oh," Mary exclaimed, realization dawning. Her fingers went to cover her mouth. "I misunderstood," she said, removing her hand. "So, where is she?"

Amelia turned and extended her hands, palms up, pointing with both hands joined together, in Minuette's direction. "Allow me to introduce you to Madam Minuette Notette de La Pointierre."

Mary's eyes widened in astonishment as she turned her gaze toward Minuette.

Minuette, having grasped the situation and comprehending some of what had been said, extended her hand in a polite greeting. "I am Minuette Notette de La Pointierre. It is a pleasure to meet you," she expressed in slightly halting English.

In her state of confusion, Mary had mixed up her inflections and inadvertently turned her greeting into a question. "It's a pleasure to meet you, madam?" she asked, her hand stopping midway toward Minuette's waiting one.

She let her hand fall to her side and gave Minuette another inquisitive once-over before turning back to Amelia. "I think I need to excuse myself. We can catch up later during the party."

The remainder of the gathering unfolded similarly, marked by covert, hushed conversations and lingering glances, accompanied by other impolite actions. As she strolled through the adjacent garden, conversations would falter in her presence, the hushed tones dissipating like morning mist, and groups would disband, scattering like leaves in the wind.

At one moment, Minuette observed Elizabeth exhibiting a faint smile during a minor incident involving a waiter. The waiter inadvertently skipped Minuette, because she was a person of color, while distributing small sandwiches. Minuette noticed Elizabeth's deliberate decision not to rectify the error, allowing the waiter to continue to the next table.

It was Amelia who eventually corrected the oversight. This, while the other ladies present observed the situation with evident and undisguised contempt in their eyes for Minuette. The other ladies, in a subtle display of their reluctance, declined to share a tray Minuette had selected from, prompting the waiter to discreetly withdraw the tray and request a fresh one from the kitchen.

This is what happened to lead Minuette into wanting to leave the American colonies. She found herself daydreaming about scenes from her home. She had little purpose or necessity for being in the American colonies. All the business decisions fell under Louis's jurisdiction. He managed the family's sugar export operations from back on their plantation in Martinique, which extended to their dealings in Savannah. Louis had no requirement for her presence in the American colonies as he efficiently oversaw the company alongside his partner, George.

At 14, Clauvère was to be considered a man due to his noble heritage. He no longer needed guidance from his mother. She saw no need for her to remain longer in the American colonies. While she cherished her son, she had witnessed his growth in the few years that they had been there and what she saw was the development of a remarkable young man that was more than capable of taking care of himself, even at such a young age.

Yet, this longing became a source of conflict, for her husband, Louis, held a different vision for their future. He loved Minuette deeply and was resolute about their life in this new land. The thought of her leaving, abandoning their family to return to the familiar shores of the French West Indies, was almost too much for him to bear.

In their conversation, conducted in rapid French, Louis expressed his concerns with a firm resolve. "I cannot bear the thought of you leaving me to return to Martinique alone. You should stay here with me. I fear someone else might steal your heart. How could you possibly go on without me?"

Minuette's hand landed gently on Louis's cheek, her touch both tender and resolute. With a deliberate slowness, she withdrew her hand, only to follow it with a swift slap to her husband's cheek, the sound amplifying the message more than the actual pain.

"Your wife is no trophy, nor some delicate trinket untouched by life's trials. You, more than anyone, understand this. You, a noble, willingly toiled in the sugar cane fields with me for a year, all in pursuit of the chance to win my heart," Minuette conveyed her feelings, a mix of love and strength evident in her words and actions.

As her internal struggle grew, Minuette finally decided to share her pain with Louis. In the intimate moments of their life together, she poured out her heart, revealing the torment she had been enduring. She narrated the constant maltreatment by Elizabeth, George's late wife's sister, who had become an unwelcome presence in her live.

With tears in her eyes, Minuette disclosed how Elizabeth had made her life, there in Savannah, miserable. Her influence extended beyond their home, poisoning the attitudes of other women in town who began to treat them with coldness and prejudice.

Louis listened, his heart breaking for the woman he cherished. It was a turning point for him as he heard about Elizabeth's frequent belittlement of Minuette during social gatherings and dinners, accusing her of arrogance and of overstepping her "negress" position.

The extent of Minuette's suffering, once unveiled, left Louis in anguish. It was then that he reached out to his close friend, George Hartford. Their bond ran deep, like brothers, and George decided to confront Elizabeth and put an end to the misery she was inflicting on Minuette.

In the serene parlor of the Hartford's home, a tense conversation ensued between George and Elizabeth. The dim light cast an aura of seriousness as George addressed her, his voice firm.

"Elizabeth, we must talk about your behavior towards the La Pointierres, particularly Minuette. Your actions have caused her immense pain, and it needs to stop."

Elizabeth, who had carried herself with an air of entitlement, reacted defensively. "Why should I change anything? They don't belong here, George. It's as simple as that."

George's patience was wearing thin, and he spoke firmly, his eyes unwavering. "Elizabeth, this goes beyond simple disapproval. Your actions are tearing our families apart, creating divisions where there shouldn't be any. We must treat the La Pointierres with respect, just as we expect to be treated."

Elizabeth, her face twisted with anger, couldn't comprehend George's position. "So, you're taking their side now? Choosing them over your own people?"

The confrontation had set new dynamics in motion. Elizabeth's anger blazed, convinced that George's actions aligned him against his own kind. It marked the beginning of a deeper clash that threatened to disrupt the delicate balance between acceptance and prejudice within the household.

Clauvère keenly observed his mother's struggles. The late-night conversations between his parents had not escaped his notice. As he lay in bed before drifting into slumber, the hushed exchanges from the adjoining room reached his ears, though he couldn't decipher their content through the separating walls.

While the sounds of insects outside filled the room, Clauvère's mind was preoccupied with finding a way to bring joy to his mother's life. Gradually, his contemplations led to a decisive plan—one that not only aimed to lift his mother's spirits but also offered a chance to redeem the honor he had lost in his previous dealings with the candy store proprietor.

With a satisfied smile, Clauvère finalized the details of his scheme, and that night, sleep embraced him with a contented grin.

The following day, with the arrival of Thibault and Peter, Clauvère set his plans into motion. In a mere two days, he had masterfully acquired the targeted store, orchestrating the dismissal of the previous proprietor with finesse and success.

The memory of the proprietor's astonishment when Clauvère entered with the store's deed in hand was etched in his mind. He had tapped into his meticulously saved allowance to make the purchase, for the store had come at the price of six hundred and seventy pounds sterling, and the previous owner had swiftly honored his note.

To ensure a smooth transaction and address his concerns about potential racial bias, Clauvère had enlisted Thibault and Peter as his representatives. They assumed his identity and conducted the business on his behalf, effectively securing the store in his name.

The following day, Clauvère unveiled the candy store to his mother, now the proud proprietor. He presented her with her favorite sweets, hoping to bring a smile to her face. Minuette, touched by the gesture, graciously accepted the gifts, expressing her gratitude with a warm smile, an affectionate hug, and a loving kiss.

With Louis's unwavering support and Clauvère's gentle encouragement, Minuette assumed the responsibilities of running the candy store. As days turned into weeks, Clauvère couldn't help but notice the shifting emotions in his mother's eyes—not toward ease or contentment, but toward something quieter and more carefully guarded. One evening, as they sat together in their home, waiting for the return of her husband, he resolved to address the issue that weighed on her heart.

"Maman," he began in French, the language of their comfort and intimacy, "Te sens-tu bien?" (Are you feeling well?)

Minuette turned her gaze toward Clauvère, a weariness evident in her eyes, though she made an attempt to mask it with a fragile smile. "Je vais bien, mon cher fils. Mes actions vous ont-elles inquiété?" (I'm fine, my dear son. Have my actions given you cause for concern?)"

Clauvère felt compelled to challenge the issue head on but at the last moment, sighed and looked down at the tea cup in his hands. He asked after something else. "Non, maman, tu ne m'as causé aucun souci." (No, mother, you haven't caused me any concern.) Clauvère lifted his face to regard his mother. With a smile he asked, "Comment est le magasin?" (How is the store?)

Minuette frowned momentarily, thinking whether or not she should burden her son with news of the store. She finally settled her conflict by deciding that he was a growing young man who needed to know. She decided to give her son the truth.

"Les choses allaient bien au début. Les clients qui fréquentaient à l'origine le magasin sous l'ancien propriétaire revenaient sans cesse." (Things were going well at the beginning. The customers who originally had frequented the store under the old ownership continued to come back.) she said.

Minuette paused. She knew she was at the challenging part of her revelation and knew that it might cause problems for Clauvère to reveal the rest. "Lorsque les clients se sont rendu compte que le magasin appartenait désormais à une personne de couleur, la clientèle s'est réduite à néant." (As the customers became aware that the store was now owned by a person of color, the clientele thinned out to nothing.)

Minuette let out a heavy sigh and turned her gaze toward the expansive bay window. With a deep breath, she spoke, "Le confiseur qui travaillait pour l'ancien propriétaire nous a informé qu'il ne pouvait plus produire nos confiseries. Je crains que nous devions envisager de fermer le magasin ou de le mettre en vente." (The candy maker who used to work for the previous owner informed us that he can no longer produce our confections. I'm afraid we might have to consider closing the shop or putting it up for sale.)

A month later, they made the difficult decision to sell the store. Their attempt to address the problem by hiring white individuals to oversee the daily operations had also proven unsuccessful. The challenge of hiring white employees had arisen, as many declined to work for the establishment, aware of Clauvère's ownership and Minuette's management.

Minuette had finally made up her mind to depart, and nothing could sway her decision. She conveyed her determination to Louis. Penny had also come by, along with the rest of the Hartford family, to bid their farewells. After everyone had said their goodbyes, Penny remained, the last one to do so.

Penny approached Minuette slowly. She so resembled the little, small girl who hid behind her father the first time that they met. She reached out to Minuette and wrapped her arms around her. "Non, maman. You can't leave me now." In her distress, she mixed French and English.

Minuette stroked the girls cheek. She was surprised and grateful at the same time that Penny had called her mother. "Je dois partir maintenant." (I have to go now.)

She wiped the tears away from Penny's eyes. "Sois fort petit. Mon précieux enfant." (Be strong little one. My precious child.)

Penny shook her head so that her platinum tresses flowed back and forth. "Non, je ne veux pas être forte, maman. Je te veux." (No, I don't want to be strong, mother. I want you.)

Minuette lifted Penny's chin with a gentle finger. She looked at Penny's pouting, tear filled face and almost laughed. "Ouvre les yeux, mon petit, et regarde là-bas." (Open your eyes, little one, and look over there.) Minuette pointed Penny's face towards Clauvère who stood a little ways off and could not hear them. "Ce garçon navigue vers ton étoile. La seule raison pour laquelle il se lance dans ce voyage difficile est parce qu'il sait que vous êtes sa destination." (That boy sails toward your star. The only reason he is embarking on this difficult journey is because he knows you are his destination.)

Minuette hugged Penny tightly. "Go to him and guide him," she said.

Minuette redirected her attention to her husband, Louis, and in her melodic native French accent, she spoke, "I will entrust our son to you, Louis. Please, take good care of him. I know that he is struggling here, just as I am, but he is also growing stronger."

She kissed Louis on both cheeks and held his hands tenderly in her own. Louis gently turned her gaze back toward their son, mirroring the shift in his own eyes. "He is blossoming into a remarkable young man. I can see he has found purpose along the way," he said with a smile, his thoughts drifting to the influence of Penny on their son's growth.

The day was sweltering, the air thick with anticipation and fear, as Minuette, matron of the La Pointierre family, prepared to depart Savannah for the French West Indies. Clauvère's family had made the painful decision, letting Minuette leave the colonies at this time. A Revolutionary War loomed ever closer in the American colonies as political tensions within the Americas grew stronger. Louis and Clauvère hoped for the safety of the wife and mother in the Caribbean. The threat of conflict could potentially extend to the relative safety of that tropical land, for the Caribbean served as a crucial launching point for British forces into the American colonies.

Clauvère stood on the dock next to the ship, watching the bustling port of Savannah unfold around him. His mother, Minuette, had held his hand tightly before she boarded the ship. Her eyes seemed to reflect the uncertainty that lay ahead. Letting her leave their newfound home was a painful choice, but they held on to hope that they would find a better life in the West Indies for her as she returned to their sugar plantation.

CHEVALIER
LOUIS JEAN-BAPTISTE
de LA POINTIERRE

PART THREE

8

The Hartford estate bustled with a peculiar tension. It was the year 1773. Minuette had only been gone a few weeks and Elizabeth's presence was causing problems. Additionally, a heavy cloud of unrest had descended upon the American colonies, casting its long shadow even over the tranquility of the Hartford household.

Amid the quaint and sunlit backdrop of their home, tensions simmered beneath the surface, perpetuated by the unwelcome influence of Elizabeth, George's persistent and traditional-minded sister-in-law. It was her relentless insistence that had led to a decision that would forever change their lives — Minuette de La Pointierre's departure from Savannah.

The atmosphere had grown oppressive, with Elizabeth's constant complaints echoing through the corridors. She declared that she needed help around the house. George found himself grappling with this new reality, Elizabeth's presence shifting the dynamics in the house in unpredictable ways.

In the elegant parlor of the Hartford mansion, George was engaged in a heated discussion with his sister-in-law, Elizabeth. The room's pristine white walls, adorned with portraits of ancestors, seemed to reflect their shared familial past. However, the present was a different story.

"George, you must do something about the servants," Elizabeth implored, her tone laced with desperation. Her blue eyes were wide, reflecting the anxiety she felt. "They've been leaving in droves, and none are willing to be hired to work under me. You know how crucial it is for the Hartford name to maintain its standing in this society."

George sighed, his broad shoulders heavy with responsibility. He understood the importance of preserving the Hartford legacy, especially in these tumultuous times. "I know, Elizabeth. But what do you expect me to do? The servants are leaving because of the rumors and whispers spreading through the town about your treatment of them."

Their conversation reached a standstill and Elizabeth left in a huff. George went to sit down, his hand holding his head as his elbow rested upon the surface of the desk. He groaned aloud and was surprised when a knock at the doorframe of his study caught his attention.

A familiar figure entered the room. It was Jeremiah, one of the long-standing servants who had decided to part ways with the Hartford estate. His face was etched with a sense of determination and resolve as he approached George.

"Mr. Hartford," Jeremiah began, his voice tinged with sympathy, "I wanted to speak with you about my decision to leave. It's not about you, sir, but the situation in this house."

George nodded, understanding that the servant's departure was a result of the pervasive rumors and the darkening cloud of unrest surrounding Elizabeth's treatment of the help. "I know it's not personal, Jeremiah. Tell me, what has driven you to make this choice?"

Jeremiah hesitated for a moment, choosing his words carefully. "It's Mrs. Salisbury, Mr. Hartford. Word has been spreading like wildfire. They say it's best not to work for the Hartford home anymore. The tensions working under her are high, and folks fear getting caught in the crossfire between you and Mrs. Salisbury."

George clenched his fists, his heart heavy with disappointment. The loyalty of long-standing servants was integral to the Hartford estate's reputation, and now it was crumbling before him. "I understand, Jeremiah. I can't fault you for prioritizing yourself."

Jeremiah nodded, his eyes expressing gratitude. "I wish you luck, Mr. Hartford. I hope things turn around for your family. The Hartford name has been respected in this town for generations, and it would be a shame to see it tarnished."

As Jeremiah made his exit, George was left to ponder the immense challenges that lay ahead. The Hartford estate felt suddenly hollow — not merely understaffed, but wounded. Jeremiah had not left alone; his wife, once the quiet anchor of the kitchen, had gone with him.

George had always avoided the idea of hiring indentured servants. The arrangement sat poorly with him — too close to coercion, too far from the mutual respect he believed a household should be built upon. Yet circumstances pressed in on him from all sides.

At last, worn thin by necessity, George relented — not by hiring anyone just yet, but by accepting that he would have to.

The following morning, he ventured into the bustling city, a mix of trepidation and reluctant resolve in his heart, intent on finding help where he could — even if it meant crossing a line he had long resisted.

With a sense of urgency, George made his way to a nearby agency, determined to find a solution to the growing void within the Hartford home. The aroma of roasted coffee beans wafted through the air as he entered the agency's elegant foyer, a stark contrast to the looming problems he hoped to address.

Seated there, in the hushed lobby, he waited with an air of restrained patience. The fine upholstery of the waiting room chairs was at odds with the desperation he felt. It was here that he anticipated his meeting with the agency's representative, who he hoped would offer a lifeline in their time of need.

George's wait was not overly lengthy, as the agency's efficient staff soon directed him to a private office. He stepped inside to find a neatly dressed agent behind a mahogany desk, meticulously arranging a stack of papers. The agent looked up with a welcoming smile as George entered, and after brief introductions, they dived into the matter at hand.

"I need help, sir," George explained with a tone of urgency. "Our kitchen staff has been dwindling, and we're in dire need of someone to fill the void. A trusted servant and his wife left recently, and the word has spread that nobody wants to work for the Hartfords. We can't manage the household without proper assistance."

The agent listened attentively, nodding sympathetically as George recounted the predicament. After a thoughtful pause, he said, "I understand your situation, Mr. Hartford. We can certainly assist you in finding suitable help. However, in light of the recent challenges, I should mention that there might be a premium on hiring skilled domestic workers."

George understood the implication at once. It wasn't that skilled domestic workers were scarce — it was that few were willing to enter a household where Elizabeth presided. Those who remained willing knew their leverage, and they priced it accordingly. Negotiations ensued, and after a brief but spirited discussion, they arrived at an agreed-upon price. George knew it was a significant commitment, but he was willing to pay the cost to ensure his household ran smoothly.

With the financial aspects settled, the agent rose from his desk, offering George a reassuring smile. "Now, Mr. Hartford, I'd like to introduce you to someone who I believe will be of great assistance to your household. Her name is Homily."

As he spoke, the agent opened the office door, revealing a young black girl standing in the corridor. Homily appeared to be in her teens, her dark eyes filled with a mix of curiosity and apprehension. Dressed neatly, she carried herself with a quiet dignity that hinted at a resilient spirit.

George extended his hand to greet her, responsibility heavy on his shoulders. "Homily, it's a pleasure to meet you. I hope you'll find a welcoming home in our service."

When George acquired Homily, he was adamant about one thing – the indentured servant would be under the care of his daughter, Amelia. He wouldn't allow Elizabeth to have more power than she already possessed. He laid down the rules firmly, informing her that Homily would be confined to the kitchen, tasked solely with cooking and cleaning thereof.

Elizabeth's anger flared, a storm of displeasure she directed at George. She had hoped for more, but her brother-in-law's decision left her bitter and frustrated.

The Hartford household turmoil was far from over. Elizabeth's ambitions turned towards Penelope, the quiet and mysterious girl who refused to speak in English to anyone other than Clauvère. The unspoken tension had swelled like a gathering storm.

Penny found solace in the presence of Clauvère, savoring the memory of summoning the courage to reveal her long-held emotions not too long ago. The celebration was two-fold, as Clauvère had confessed his feelings in return. She couldn't help but feel that he, too, must be elated right then at being with her, especially considering how Elizabeth had tried to keep them apart.

However, she couldn't ignore the shadow of concern that seemed to have enveloped Clauvère. There were moments when he appeared lost in his thoughts but not like this. Even during their walks in the nearby garden or woods, he would seem distracted, his attention not wholly on her. He would comment on their surroundings or engage in conversations with her and Peter about city events. Everything he said and did appeared to contribute to his pursuit of a specific goal. Penelope wasn't oblivious to this. Most, if not all, of his actions seemed directed toward securing a future with her, not just in the present.

Clauvère, who cherished Penelope's company and held the same affection in his heart, found himself discouraged as he continued to witness the injustices faced by black individuals in the colonies, even when they were free.

Life in Savannah had increasingly presented itself as a formidable challenge, one that he tackled head-on. Despite his unwavering determination, George encountered obstacles in rallying support for his efforts to effect change. His venture into the store business had proven lackluster, and though he took satisfaction in exacting retribution on the proprietor, thus restoring his honor by dismissing the man, it offered little respite for his enduring concerns. Paradoxically, owning the shop merely deepened his disillusionment with the prevailing social norms of the era, given its struggle to attract customers who were reluctant to patronize an establishment owned by black individuals.

His reverie was gently interrupted by a soft voice. Penelope, her tone tender, inquired, "à quoi pensez-vous, monseigneur?" (What are you thinking about, My Lord?)

Clauvère, who had been gazing at the sky, slowly turned to meet Penelope's eyes. "Nothing," he replied as he extended his hand to grasp hers.

He then turned his gaze back towards the horizon, speaking so softly that Penelope had to lean in to hear him clearly. "I feel the winds of change flowing. The breeze seems to be getting stronger."

But before Penelope could seek further clarity, Elizabeth intervened. She approached them, her posture haughty, and cast a disapproving glance at their clasped hands.

In a stern tone, Elizabeth initiated the conversation. "Penelope," she began, "I believe it's time for our guest to leave. The afternoon is waning, and you have your knitting to attend to." With that declaration, she pivoted on her heels and walked away, leaving Clauvère without acknowledgment.

As her aunt departed, Penelope rose from her seat and responded, "Oui, tante Elizabeth," (Yes, Aunt Elizabeth.) to her aunt's retreating form.

Elizabeth halted in her tracks, pivoting to face Penelope. She sighed in evident frustration. "I do wish you would communicate in English. You know I can't understand a word of that language you are speaking." Elizabeth intentionally avoided naming the language, a tactic seemingly aimed at dismissing Clauvère's presence, before she continued her departure.

Penny turned to Clauvère before she too left. She confessed to Clauvère, her voice a gentle whisper, "Je vous aime, Mon Seigneur. Quand nous serons plus grands, nous nous marierons." (I love you, My Lord. When we're older, we'll get married.)

Over the last few winters, Penelope had spent countless hours learning French from Clauvère. Her dedication was unwavering, and she had blossomed into a fluent speaker. While she spoke both English and French with Clauvère and his mother, Minuette Notette, she would only converse in French with anyone else, and only when they were at home.

This behavior frustrated Elizabeth to no end, and she constantly prodded George to put an end to it. However, George found Penelope's linguistic skills amusing and chose not to discourage her, further deepening the divide between him and his sister-in-law.

Penelope remained steadfast in her refusal to speak outside the confines of her home as well. She was a girl of few words in the presence of others, adhering to her own unique set of rules in a world defined by its limitations and prejudices.

Penny sat at her small writing desk, pencil in hand, trying to capture her thoughts on paper. When Penny found herself alone in her room that night, she discerned the faint sound of footsteps in the hallway, which she suspected belonged to Homily. The footsteps she heard in the corridor drew her attention away from her task. She glanced towards the door, and when it creaked open, there stood Homily, still hesitant.

Penny, having looked up from her notes, her eyes brightening with a warm smile, said, "Homily, please come in," she beckoned gently. "I've been wanting to talk to you." She hurried to her door and extended a warm invitation to the girl, encouraging her to step inside for a conversation.

Penny's room was bathed in the glow of the moon and candlelight, casting long shadows on the polished wooden floor.

Homily had been laboring in their household for several days, and Penny realized that she hadn't yet had the opportunity to speak with the girl, who happened to be her own age. She was eager to rectify this and get to know Homily better.

Homily initially expressed reservations, emphasizing her status as an indentured servant and the accompanying restrictions. "Oh, Miss Penelope, I'm just an indentured servant. We're not supposed to..."

However, Penny dismissed these concerns, clearly conveying her determination to establish a genuine friendship with Homily through their conversation.

She cut in, her enthusiasm unwavering. "Nonsense! Titles and rules don't matter here. We're just two girls, and I'd love to get to know you better. Have a seat, please."

Homily shifted on her feet, her apprehension apparent in her eyes.

Homily couldn't help but ease into a hesitant but genuine smile. "Well, if you say so, Miss Penelope."

Penelope gestured to the chair across from her. "It's not Miss Penelope when we're alone. You can just call me Penny. So, Homily, tell me about yourself. How did you end up here in Savannah?"

Homily found herself drawn to the offered seat, curiosity overcoming her initial reluctance. "I came from Charleston," she began, her voice growing steadier. "My family couldn't afford to take care of me, and they said I'd have better opportunities working as an indentured servant. So, I signed the contract."

Penny's eyes reflected sympathy as she listened to Homily's story. But she also realized that there was an underlying truth in that story that Homily wasn't revealing. It was something in the way that her hands twisted together as she spoke of how she became an indentured servant that gave her away to Penny.

Penny chose not to comment on it and said instead, "That must have been so hard," she acknowledged. "How do you like it here at the Hartford estate?"

Homily considered the question carefully, her gaze moving to the sunlit window. "It's different from what I expected. I've heard stories about the Hartfords, but working for your family isn't as bad as the rumors. I'm grateful for that."

Penny leaned in, her enthusiasm evident. "I'm glad to hear that! If you have any questions or need anything, don't hesitate to ask. We'll make sure you're comfortable here."

Gratitude filled Homily's eyes as she replied, "Thank you, Penny. You've been kinder to me than anyone else here."

Penny smiled warmly. "It's the least I can do. We're going to be friends, Homily, no matter what those rules say. What do you like to do in your free time?"

Homily's face brightened with a genuine smile. "I enjoy sewing and reading when I can. It's nice to have some moments to myself."

Penny's eyes lit up with enthusiasm. "Oh, I love sewing too! Maybe we can do it together sometime. And I have a collection of books that I think you'll enjoy. We'll find a way to make your time here more pleasant."

Touched and grateful, Homily's eyes shone with appreciation. "Thank you, Penelope. I didn't expect such kindness. I'd like that, spending time with you."

With a warm smile, Penny concluded, "Great! I think we're going to be wonderful friends, Homily." And in that moment, the two young girls found the beginnings of a unique and steadfast friendship that would weather the challenges of their time.

They conversed for an extended period, during which Homily appeared to grow increasingly at ease in Penny's company. This left Penny pondering the peculiar dynamic of how easily she had formed a connection with the young girl and could converse in English, a language she rarely used with anyone other than Clauvère, even excluding their mutual friend Peter.

Despite the warmth of their growing friendship, Penny couldn't help but feel a nagging worry about the secrets Homily might be concealing. Determined to uncover the truth, she continued to press Homily with questions until, under the gentle but persistent pressure from Penelope, the young girl finally began to open up and share her story.

In a bustling 18th-century city of Charleston, South Carolina, where the alleys were narrow and shadowed by the looming facades of colonial buildings,

Homily lived with her family. The city was known for its vibrant markets, but it was also a place where deceit and manipulation thrived in the darker corners.

Homily's father had been a skilled craftsman, known for his intricate woodwork and beautiful furniture. However, their family faced dire financial circumstances when his shop was destroyed in a devastating fire. The loss of their livelihood cast them into poverty, and they struggled to make ends meet.

It was during this time that a sinister figure, lurking in the fringes of the city, took notice of Homily's family. This shadowy character was Mr. Harkins, a manipulative and unscrupulous agent who specialized in recruiting vulnerable individuals into indentured servitude.

One fateful evening, as Homily was returning from a market with a meager load of groceries, Mr. Harkins and his associates abducted her from a quiet alley. The men were silent, and their faces were obscured beneath the hoods of their cloaks. They seized Homily with a sudden and chilling efficiency, spiriting her away to a hidden location.

Homily found herself in a dimly lit room, her heart pounding with fear and confusion. The room smelled musty, and the wooden floor creaked ominously underfoot. As her eyes adjusted to the dim light, she saw Mr. Harkins seated at a weathered wooden desk, wearing a self-satisfied grin.

With false promises and deceitful words, Mr. Harkins painted a tantalizing picture of a future for Homily. He spoke of a wealthy benefactor who needed skilled workers. He assured Homily that this benefactor would provide her with a stable job, food, shelter, and even the promise of eventual freedom.

Homily was overwhelmed by the mounting desperation of her family's situation. With the hope of securing their future, in addition to the pressure exerted by the men before her, Homily reluctantly agreed to sign a contract presented to her by Mr. Harkins. Little did she know that this contract, concealed beneath layers of misleading words and legal jargon, was in fact an indentured servitude agreement, binding her to servitude for a specified number of years.

As the quill scratched her mark against the parchment, sealing her fate, Homily was engulfed by a profound sense of dread. The truth was finally revealed when she was transported to Savannah, Georgia, where the harsh realities of her situation began to unravel before her eyes. It was a dark and unjust path that led her to the door of the Hartford estate and, eventually, to her role in the unfolding narrative.

Penny rose from her seat and gracefully crossed the room to reach Homily. With tenderness, she enveloped the young girl in a comforting embrace. "Do your parents know where you are?" she inquired, her voice gentle and concerned.

"No, I don't think they know. I'm pretty sure by now they just think I'm missing and are worried sick," Homily replied, her voice muffled as she nestled against Penny's shoulder.

Penny, her resolve unwavering, assured, "Tomorrow, we'll send them a letter by courier to let them know where you are. We'll send part of your wages to them so that they can be taken care of."

Overwhelmed by the compassion and generosity of her new friend, Homily's arms instinctively wrapped around Penny, pulling her close. "Thank you, Penny," she expressed through tears, gratitude filling her voice.

GEORGE HARTFORD

9

In the heart of Savannah, the local market thrived under the golden rays of the southern sun. On this particular day, Elizabeth, the matriarch of the Hartford family, had taken her nieces, Amelia and Penelope, to the lively market square. With no servant or slave available at their side to perform the errands, the responsibility of gathering the essentials fell squarely on the shoulders of Elizabeth and her young nieces.

Homily was promised strictly as the servant for the kitchen and Elizabeth had to live with that decree. It was a rare instance where the daily chores of a bustling market became their shared endeavor. Amelia or Penelope would usually singularly assist in this task. Now it was a task they would have to navigate together in a world marked by both tradition and the winds of change.

Tensions were running high between the Whigs and Loyalists as the American colonies moved closer to the Revolutionary War. Elizabeth had always been vocal about her Loyalist sympathies, but on this fateful day, she accidentally let slip a remark that would prove disastrous.

While perusing the market, Elizabeth engaged in a heated discussion with Amelia and especially Penny, unaware of the nearby British officer who was eavesdropping on their conversation. In her passion for the Loyalist cause, she exclaimed loudly, "These Whigs are nothing but troublemakers, and they should be put in their place."

"Aunt Elizabeth, I believe you might be taking things to an extreme," Amelia cautiously voiced her dissent, her discomfort with opposing her aunt's strong views evident.

"Young lady, you may not fully grasp the situation. Your perspective has been unduly influenced by your father's more moderate stance," countered Elizabeth.

Penny, impassioned by the cause, opted to express herself in English as she advocated for her family's beliefs. "Aunt Elizabeth, I stand by what our father advocates." This was one of the few times that she spoke in English, preferring French much more.

Amelia, caught between loyalty to her sister and a desire for balance, lent her voice to the conversation. "Indeed, Father proposes that we should seek a middle ground to resolve our issues."

Penny interjected once more, emphasizing their father's nuanced approach. "Father primarily critiques British policies and seeks a middle path that would grant greater colonial autonomy and representation within the British Empire."

Elizabeth responded with a disdainful snort. "Such words border on sedition. I, on the other hand, remain steadfast in my allegiance to the British Crown and vehemently oppose the notion of American independence. I believe in the perpetuation of British colonial rule, viewing the pursuit of independence as nothing but rebellion."

"But seeking representation in the Empire is not the same as seeking independence," Amelia retorted. "Father says that he thinks we need representation so that our voices can be heard, nothing more."

Elizabeth regarded Amelia a moment before responding. "You're right but it is still not something that loyal citizens of the Empire should be asking for. If his majesty thinks that it is right for us to have representation, he will assign someone to fulfill that responsibility. We, as commoners, have no right to impose our views on the nobility."

A patron from one of the nearby stalls cast an intrigued gaze upon Elizabeth and Penny, momentarily disrupting their conversation. "Excuse me, miss," she began, "but you and your daughters bear a striking resemblance. You're all exceptionally beautiful."

Elizabeth found herself momentarily taken aback by the unexpected comment, her cheeks flushing with a hint of embarrassment. She shifted her gaze between the kind stranger and Amelia then to Penny, whose likeness to her mother, and thus, to her aunt, was undeniable. The uncanny resemblance left no room for doubt – they shared a remarkable family resemblance. Amelia had the soft, round face of their family line while both Elizabeth and Penny possessed platinum blonde hair, though Elizabeth's had a slightly darker hue. The familial traits of high cheekbones and petite noses were clearly evident between all three of them.

Feeling a connection between them, Elizabeth extended her hand and gestured for Penny to draw closer. Penny, although somewhat hesitant, complied, mindful of her aunt's status in the household and the respect that was due to her as an elder relative. As Penny drew closer, Elizabeth turned to take Amelia's hand in her own.

Elizabeth turned and tenderly clasped Penny's hand, exuding an unexpected gentleness and warmth that momentarily took Penny by surprise. The affection conveyed in that simple gesture felt almost overwhelming to her. Then, Elizabeth did something truly astonishing, leaving Penny in a state of shock—she displayed genuine, unfeigned affection. With a delicate touch, Elizabeth smoothed the loose strands of Penny's hair away from her face, planting a kiss on her forehead before turning her attention back to the woman.

"These are the children of my late sister," Elizabeth informed the woman.

The woman responded with a thoughtful hum. "Ah, it all makes sense now."

With a cordial farewell, the woman walked away, leaving Amelia and Penny still reeling from their aunt's surprising display of affection. Unconsciously, Penny's hand reached up to touch the spot where Elizabeth's kiss had landed.

Elizabeth observed Penny's reaction, and a subtle smile tugged at the corner of her mouth. "Even though I can be strict with you two at times, you should know that I do care for the both of you," she acknowledged with a hint of sentiment. "You are my sister's children, after all." Elizabeth then turned back to the stall they had been visiting. "Now, where were we?"

Elizabeth scrutinized a display of vegetables but found it unsatisfactory before moving to the next one. "We must uphold the current colonial ties with Britain and maintain the existing social and economic structure. It's only under the Crown's protection that the rights and status of its citizens can be safeguarded."

Amelia privately mused on her aunt's unwavering stance. She silently reminded herself, "It's essential to recognize that distinctions aren't always clear-cut, and individuals often encompass a spectrum of beliefs within their respective groups. Nonetheless, Father has a point that open dialogue is crucial to prevent the impending violence in this dispute."

A short distance away, a pair of British soldiers stood near one of the stalls, their attention lingering a moment too long in Elizabeth's direction. When she noticed them and offered a polite smile in greeting, they inclined their heads in return—faces unreadable, eyes already shifting elsewhere.

Elizabeth's thoughtless comment, made in a moment of frustration, set off a chain of events that would eventually lead to the arrest of her brother-in-law,

George. She had no idea that her careless words could have far-reaching consequences for the individuals in her family.

Amelia's attention drifted again, unbidden.

She saw him then—Robert, crossing the square with two other clerks from the magistrate's office, laughing at something she could not hear. She felt the familiar impulse rise in her chest, sharp and immediate, and just as quickly pressed it down. Calling out would draw eyes. It would invite comment.

She said nothing.

Elizabeth followed the line of her gaze.

"He seems a decent young man," her aunt said after a moment, as if offering a kindness. "Steady. But decency alone does not carry one far."

Amelia turned, surprise flashing into heat. "He works. He is respected."

Elizabeth smiled faintly. "So are many men. That does not mean they are suited to the life you might have."

The words landed heavier than Amelia expected. She felt them settle, not as advice, but as judgment.

"I am not incapable of choosing for myself," she began—and stopped as Elizabeth stepped forward and drew her into an embrace.

"Hush," her aunt murmured. "I did not mean to upset you."

Amelia went still, the protest dissolving before it found shape. When Elizabeth released her, Penelope was already returning, chatter bright and unaware.

Amelia smoothed her expression and said nothing more.

It was 1773 and the revolutionary winds of dissent swept through the American colonies. The de La Pointierre family found themselves at a crossroads. Their time in the colonies had come to an end, and they made the difficult decision to return to the French West Indies and eventually move on to France itself.

It had been three years that they had spent there. Minuette had left months prior. They left behind a land on the brink of rebellion, the call of home was stronger than the uncertain path that lay ahead.

More than just the scent of an impending revolution hung heavy in the air, motivating their departure. Louis had received urgent news of his father's ailing health, compelling him to make the journey back to Pointierre, France, where his father lay bedridden. Time was of the essence, and Louis fervently hoped he would reach his father's side in time. The looming consequences of his father's potential passing weighed on him - it would thrust him into the role of the recognized ruling Count of the region, a responsibility he remained uncertain about embracing.

Penny had pestered her father to let her go to the de La Pointierre home to see Clauvère one last time before he left. George saw no reason to refuse. Even Elizabeth was somewhat supportive in her own way — she didn't protest against them meeting. That alone saved a lot of grief in the home. Amelia begged to join her sister in visiting the de La Pointierre's and was also given permission.

Amelia and Penny stood at the doorstep of the de La Pointierre home, their hearts burdened with impending goodbyes. The setting sun cast a warm, golden glow on the colonial town, a stark contrast to the turbulent winds of change sweeping through the American colonies.

Amelia nervously adjusted the bonnet that shaded her fair complexion, while Penny clutched a small bouquet of wildflowers filled with clovers, a token of farewell. The de La Pointierre family was preparing to return to the French West Indies and, ultimately, to France. Their departure left the two sisters with mixed emotions—gratitude for the friendship they had forged with Clauvère and sadness for the uncertain path ahead.

As they approached the door, Penny couldn't help but fidget with her dress. Penny recalled how she had beleaguered her father relentlessly for this visit. George, their father, understood the importance of this last meeting, recognizing Penny's need to bid farewell to Clauvère.

Upon reflecting on the events of the night she requested permission to bid farewell to Clauvère, Penny was taken aback by the unexpected compliance, even from Elizabeth, who was known for her staunch Loyalist convictions. She reminded herself of her aunt's steadfast views. Astonishingly, Elizabeth had refrained from voicing opposition to the sisters' wish to say their goodbyes. Her silence, devoid of any comment, paradoxically stood as a silent support that, for once, fostered a rare sense of harmony between them.

The door creaked open, revealing the de La Pointierre residence, a place that had seen laughter, tears, anger, shared dreams, and the forging of deep bonds. Clauvère, with a somber expression, greeted the two sisters warmly. He had always been a source of fascination for Penny, with his tales of far-off places and dreams of finding equality. But now, there was a bittersweet reality they had to confront.

As Clauvère gracefully entered the entryway hall, Penny observed his entrance. Her smile extended warmly as he approached, reaching out with both hands. What didn't escape her attention was that, as the host welcoming the Hartford family, Clauvère had overlooked the customary courtesy of greeting the head of the family first, preceding his welcome to Penelope.

Penny extended her hands to Clauvère, welcoming the gentle kisses he placed on each cheek as a greeting. Cradled in the crook of her arms rested the bouquet of wildflowers and clovers.

"Mon amour. Ma belle et chanceuse Penny," (My love. My beautiful, lucky Penny.) Clauvère whispered tenderly.

Even George couldn't help but blush, recognizing the newfound suavity of the young man.

"Monseigneur, Chevalier Clauvère. Mon Clauvère à quatre feuilles," (My Lord, Chevalier Clauvère. My four leaf Clauvère) Penny began as she curtsied.

Louis gracefully entered the area, his arms outstretched to embrace George warmly in greeting. After kissing both of George's cheeks, he stepped back, his hand still resting on George's shoulder as he observed Clauvère and Penny standing together. They seemed entirely absorbed in each other, oblivious to their surroundings. In that moment, nothing else held any significance.

Leaning in closely to George, Louis grinned. "She doesn't even call me 'My Lord,' and I'm next in line to inherit the title of Count."

Their laughter filled the moment.

"That young man is destined to change the world," George remarked, his gaze still fixed on the young couple. He turned to Louis, locking eyes with him. "They love each other. It pains me to see them separated like this."

George's head lowered as his eyes drifted to the ground. His thoughts about the future for these two youngsters were clouded by the challenges they'd face to make their relationship work and gain acceptance. His hand instinctively moved to his chin as he sought comfort in the gesture. "Perhaps, it's for the best.

They'd never be able to build a life together. A young mulatto and a white girl? No one would accept it here."

"I don't know..." Louis started, his hand slipping away from George's shoulder and crossing over his chest. "I have a feeling these two will discover the happiness they seek together. He's not striving for growth just to give up."

Penny gazed deeply into Clauvère's eyes, her cheeks flushing as tears welled up in the corners of her eyes. Her voice quivered with emotion as she spoke, "Nous ne pouvions pas supporter de vous voir partir sans vous dire au revoir, Mon Seigneur." (We couldn't bear to see you leave without saying goodbye, My Lord.)

Amelia nodded in agreement, her eyes glistening with unshed tears. "You've been a dear friend to us, and we'll never forget the times we've shared."

Clauvère, though sad to part ways, managed a wistful smile. "I'll never forget the two of you either. You've brought a piece of the colonies into my heart, and I'll carry it with me wherever I go."

The conversation flowed, punctuated by shared memories, laughter, and a few tears. They spoke of the uncertain future, their hopes, and the bonds that would withstand time and distance.

As the sun dipped below the horizon during their heartfelt farewell, Clauvère extended a gleaming penny toward Penny. He explained that he had kept one for himself too, not as a mere token of friendship, but as a keepsake to remember her by while he embarked on his uncertain journey. The exchanged pennies, symbols of their shared moments, became treasures to hold onto in the face of the parting that the winds of change had imposed upon them.

In a reciprocal gesture of their unspoken bond, Penny handed Clauvère the bouquet of wildflowers she had picked earlier, now adorned with vibrant clovers. Each blossom and clover was a silent wish, a promise of hope and friendship, carefully woven into the fabric of their parting. The exchange of these simple yet heartfelt tokens solidified the connection between them, transcending the physical distance that would soon separate their paths.

As they exchanged these meaningful tokens, Clauvère held the clover-studded bouquet close to his heart, while Penny clutched the gleaming penny with a sense of cherished connection. In these small mementos, they found solace and a reminder of the enduring bond that transcended the impending distance. Clauvère had his 'clover,' and Penny had her 'penny'—symbols of their lasting friendship and the hope of reunions yet to come.

Penny, with a heavy heart, finally said, "Même si nos chemins se séparent maintenant, je suis convaincu que nos chemins se croiseront à nouveau un jour." (Though we part ways now, I have no doubt our paths will cross again someday.)

Clauvère inhaled deeply, his shoulders trembling as emotions tightened their grip. "I'll never leave you behind. I'm fighting to achieve my dreams, and I have just one dream."

Penny blinked back tears, and Clauvère's hand gently rose to wipe away what her own efforts couldn't. "Quel rêve faites-vous, Mon Seigneur?" (What dream do you have, My Lord?) she asked, her voice soft.

A smile graced Clauvère's face. "The dream I have is of you."

Penny's eyes shimmered with tears as she responded to Clauvère's heartfelt words. Her hand moved to rest on his cheek. She whispered, her voice filled with poignant tenderness, "Ton rêve est le mien aussi, mon amour. Monseigneur." (Your dream is mine as well, my love. My Lord.)

Amelia, Penny, and Clauvère shared a final embrace, a silent promise of future reunions. As they walked away from the de La Pointierre home, they couldn't help but glance back one last time at the house that had been a sanctuary of friendship and understanding. The revolutionary winds, the social injustices, the stratification of hierarchy, may have blown them apart for now, but their bond remained unbroken, a testament to the enduring power of friendship and the strength to face an uncertain future.

As Clauvère stepped onto the ship bound for Martinique alongside his father, his thoughts inevitably drifted to Penny. He had arrived in the summer of 1770 at the tender age of twelve. Now, in the autumn of 1773, he was bidding farewell to the life he had carefully constructed in this foreign land. A tear welled up in the corner of his eye and trailed down his cheek, for he was acutely aware that, in leaving, he was also leaving behind the most significant part of his "life," the girl who had touched his heart so deeply—Penny.

Clauvère extended his hand, his fingers curling into a determined fist. He made a solemn vow to himself, pledging that he would pursue his dream with unwavering resolve. Someday, he envisioned a future where he could openly declare his feelings for Penny to the world without hesitation or restraint. He yearned for the day when they could embrace their love both in the intimate moments of privacy and the unyielding light of public acceptance.

The Hartford family arrived back home that evening while George held his crying daughter in his arms. Amelia strove her best not to shed tears for the loss of someone she considered a friend. Over the years of tutoring Clauvère, she had grown fond of him and of his family. The closeness the two families shared couldn't be denied. It was a loss felt by all of them, excluding Elizabeth.

Elizabeth still harbored complicated feelings about the de La Pointierre family, particularly their son Clauvère. Even so, she could not ignore Penelope's grief. She, too, had known the pain of loss. Her heart had been wounded twice—first by George when he chose her sister over her, and again by her husband, who had passed away less than a year ago.

On the night of Clauvère's departure, Elizabeth set aside her reservations and became a source of comfort for both girls as they grappled with their sorrow. Whatever doubts lingered within her—shaped by habit, tradition, and long-held prejudice—remained unspoken. In the warm glow of the parlor, she sat with them on the couch, the girls flanking her on either side, offering the only solace she knew how to give.

Seated in the parlor, Elizabeth found herself ensnared in the web of conflicting emotions, a delicate dance between reservations and genuine empathy. The warm glow of the room seemed to amplify the dichotomy playing out within her.

Her reservations about Clauvère's family, a product of societal expectations and ingrained biases, whispered like shadows in the corners of her mind. The familiar tug of tradition sought to restrain her, to confine her judgment within the parameters of societal norms. It was a struggle against the currents of ingrained beliefs that warred with the evolving landscape of her emotions.

Yet, as Penelope and Amelia flanked her on either side, their grief palpable in the quietude of the parlor, Elizabeth did what she could for the girls who were enveloped in the vulnerability of their mourning.

Conflict raged though. She shook her head clear of the clash of societal expectations and an evolving understanding of compassion. Elizabeth understood that empathy could coexist with reservations, that the rigid lines drawn by society might blur in the face of genuine human connection. But that didn't mean she could readily accept it so easily.

As the flickering flames cast shadows on the walls, Elizabeth's internal dialogue unfolded—a complex interplay of tradition and compassion, resistance and understanding. The parlor, a microcosm of societal expectations, became the arena where Elizabeth wrestled with the intricacies of her own beliefs, navigating the delicate balance between tradition and the human capacity for empathy.

Observing this tender scene, George acknowledged Elizabeth's capacity for such compassion—a trait that could undoubtedly captivate any man. However, he understood that despite the endearing qualities she possessed, he could never offer her his heart. Drifting away from the poignant tableau, he continued through the house, briefly pausing to witness the moment before disappearing into his personal study. Behind closed doors, he immersed himself in the solitude of the room, taking measured sips of a dark drink, contemplating the complexities of the relationships around him.

George sank into the worn leather chair, a heavy silence enveloping the room. The dim glow of the solitary lamp cast long shadows, amplifying the cost of his responsibilities as the head of the household. His mind, a canvas of contemplation, painted a mosaic of emotions and uncertainties.

He turned the facets of his thoughts towards his daughters, each a unique thread weaving the complex tapestry of his life. Amelia's development into a young woman of marriageable age harkened a departure from the family. A pursuit, for her, of a life beyond the familiar walls that would leave a void, and an indication of the inevitability of change. Penelope's growing attachment to Clauvère, once a subtle undertone, now resonated loudly in the chambers of his reflections.

The de La Pointierre's departure lingered in the air like a melody that had abruptly ceased, leaving behind an echo of unspoken words and unrealized potential. The family's presence and Louis had been a constant for the last few years, a force that transcended the boundaries of societal expectations. George pondered the impact of this absence, the void it left not only in his daughters' lives but in his own.

The memory of his late wife hovered, a specter of feminine presence he could no longer provide to his growing daughters. The ache of her absence intertwined with the contemplation of the recent departure, a poignant reminder of the irrevocable changes life had imposed.

The dark drink in his hand, a companion to his introspection, mirrored the shadows that danced across his mind. Each sip was a pause, a moment to grapple with the uncharted territory of his own emotions. George found solace in the liquid's bitter embrace, a tangible reminder of the complexities that defined his role as a father, a provider, and a man navigating the currents of change.

In the stillness of the study, George acknowledged the duality of his emotions—the pride in his daughters' blossoming independence and the pang of uncertainty that accompanied the shifting dynamics. The dark drink, now diminished, held the residue of contemplation, the ongoing journey of self-discovery in the ever-evolving narrative of his life.

Back in the parlor, Amelia's mind echoed with a lingering sense of helplessness as she recalled the door closing behind the departing de La Pointierre family. Their absence left a void, a stark reminder that her world had shifted. The familiar walls of her family home seemed to close in, and she grappled with the realization that change had become an undeniable force.

Over the years, watching Clauvère navigate the tumultuous currents of his own aspirations had been a revelation. In his struggles, she found a mirror reflecting the potential for transformation within herself. His determination to shape his destiny, regardless of societal expectations, resonated deeply with her. It was a poignant realization—Clauvère's presence had become a catalyst for her own metamorphosis.

She thought of the market—how easily Penny's passion had been forgiven, while her own careful words had been corrected. How often she was reminded to temper herself, to soften her thoughts before giving them voice. Penny was allowed to feel. Amelia was expected to understand—quietly.

As she contemplated the constraints society imposed on women, Amelia recognized the parallel between Clauvère's defiance of racial boundaries and her own potential to challenge the limitations imposed on her gender. The societal norms that dictated a woman's path were formidable, yet she found courage in Clauvère's example.

Sitting in the quiet aftermath, she pondered the sacrifices required for such a struggle. Societal expectations pressed down on her, but the ember of determination sparked by Clauvère's journey flickered within. The path to forging her own destiny was fraught with challenges, but the fire of inspiration burned bright.

In the tapestry of her thoughts, Amelia recognized the need to redefine her place in a world that had suddenly become more expansive. The departure of the de La Pointierre family was not just an end but a beginning—an invitation to challenge norms, break free from constraints, and embark on a journey of self-discovery. The echoes of Clauvère's resilience whispered through her contemplations, fueling her resolve to confront the societal boundaries that sought to confine her.

As night descended, Amelia retreated to her room, having exhausted the reservoir of fleeting emotions that required consolation. The tears shed, grief acknowledged, and solace received, she accepted the departure of the de La Pointierre family. Fatigue settled over her, prompting the need for rest. Meanwhile, Penny remained steadfast by her aunt's side, enveloped in tender reassurances that life would eventually resume its normal course.

Penny's turbulent thoughts surged like a tempest within her. The warmth of her aunt's embrace provided a momentary sanctuary, yet her mind was a cacophony of conflicting emotions, a whirlwind of uncertainties.

As she sought solace in the familiar contours of Elizabeth's presence, the only feminine presence in her life now that her mother was gone, Penny questioned the depth of her aunt's comprehension. Could Elizabeth truly fathom the intricacies of the emotions that tethered her heart to Clauvère? The societal barriers loomed large, casting shadows on the connection that had blossomed amidst the serenity of their shared time together over the years. It was a love that transcended conventions, a sentiment she yearned for Elizabeth to understand. The distance that would separate them seemed like an insurmountable obstacle that stood in her way.

The departure of the de La Pointierre family echoed in her thoughts like a haunting melody, intensifying the sense of isolation that had become an unwelcome companion. In Clauvère's absence, Penny grappled with the solitude, a loneliness that reverberated through the corners of her heart.

The uncertainty of her own future loomed like an ominous cloud on the horizon. Questions danced in her mind, each step into the unknown echoing with the resounding 'what ifs' that plagued her contemplation. Would her path align with Clauvère's, or would societal expectations and distance dictate a different course?

Amidst the tender assurances whispered by Elizabeth, Penny's thoughts were a tapestry woven with threads of love, barriers, and the uncharted territories of her emotions. In the cocoon of her aunt's arms, she yearned for understanding, a connection that could bridge the gap between societal norms, distance and the beating of her own heart.

Nestled in Elizabeth's arms, Penny ventured, "Aunt Elizabeth, have you ever loved someone so deeply that it hurt this much when they weren't there?"

Elizabeth considered the question, her thoughts echoing, 'Yes, child. Twice. One of those men was your father.' Yet, she chose to keep these sentiments unspoken. Instead, she shared, "You forget that I was married before I came here. I loved your uncle very much and was devastated when he passed away."

As Elizabeth contemplated the individual who held Penny's affections, she grappled with her disapproval of the interracial nature of the relationship. Despite this, she recognized the universal pain of losing a loved one. Reflecting on the boy, she acknowledged his nobility and begrudgingly admired his strength. Memories of their initial meeting and subsequent interactions at the de La Pointierre's household led Elizabeth to a reluctant acknowledgment—he was destined for greatness.

"Life sometimes throws us challenges that we must overcome. I'm sure that with time, this pain will lessen, Penelope," Elizabeth reassured. She drew Penny even closer, planting a kiss on the top of her head. Penny reciprocated by wrapping her arms around her aunt, seeking comfort and warmth in Elizabeth's words and presence.

Elizabeth felt a sense of contentment as Penny sought solace from her. What brought even greater joy was that Penny had chosen to converse in English, a voluntary first for her. Elizabeth observed Penny, noticing the signs of drowsiness—her eyes drifting closed, the quieting of sobs. Standing, Elizabeth gently guided her niece to the room. There, she assisted Penny in changing into night clothes, brushed her hair with tender care, and tucked her in. A gentle kiss on Penny's forehead marked the end of this nightly ritual, and Elizabeth headed to her own room to prepare for the night.

In the aftermath of the girls retiring, the soft sighs of the settling night permeated the air, underscoring the stillness of the house. Elizabeth found herself grappling with the echoes of loneliness reverberating through the empty spaces around her, the quiet seeming to magnify the void that lingered in the corners of each room. After nearly fifteen minutes of restlessness, sleep remained elusive. Reluctantly, she rose and descended to the kitchen for a drink.

As Elizabeth wandered through the dimly lit halls, moonlight filtered through the curtains, painting the walls in silver and casting elongated shadows that shifted with each step. Memories of her own losses resurfaced like ghosts from the past. The specter of her late husband — and the man she had loved, now her brother-in-law — seemed to tread silently alongside her. Recollections of shared laughter and childhood warmth clashed with the stark reality of his choice: first to be with her sister until her passing, and now to remain distant, even with nothing binding either of them.

The creaking of the floorboards beneath her feet echoed through the quiet house, a subtle reminder of its age and history. Elizabeth, despite her stoic exterior, felt the pressure of everything pressing down on her. The barriers erected by tradition and expectation cast long shadows, threatening to obscure the fragile connections her niece fought to preserve with Clauvère.

In the solitude of the night, Elizabeth's thoughts turned inward, reflecting on the delicate balance between holding fast to cherished memories and navigating the forces that so often pulled people apart. The house stood silent around her, bearing witness to the ebb and flow of lives intertwined within its walls.

Passing by the parlor, she noticed George had relocated from his study and now sat watching the fire. The flames cast a warm, golden glow across the room, light and shadow playing softly along the walls. Pulling her robe tighter around herself, Elizabeth paused just inside the doorway, waiting for George to acknowledge her presence.

George glanced up from his glass, turning his gaze from the fire as he took another sip of his dark beverage. Seeing Elizabeth, he welcomed her in. "Why don't you come in and have a seat, Elizabeth," he suggested gently.

Elizabeth moved further into the dimly lit space, the fire casting flickering shadows. Seating herself on the sofa beside him, George extended a tumbler toward her, pouring brandy. The subtle aroma of brandy lingered in the air as George poured the drink. The rich, amber liquid swirled in the glass. She accepted it with both hands, taking a sip before letting the glass rest in her lap, her hands cradling it. The quiet exchange of gestures and the subdued atmosphere spoke volumes about the unspoken connection between them, punctuated by the crackling fire. The warmth radiating from the crackling fire enveloped Elizabeth and George as they sat in the parlor. The comforting heat contrasted with the cool night outside. Through the large windows, the moonlit night unfolded, bathing the surroundings in a silvery glow where the firelight failed to illuminate. The nocturnal landscape outside became a silent observer to the unfolding scene within the house.

For about another fifteen minutes, the two of them sat in companionable silence, each immersed in their own thoughts. George appeared lost in contemplation, and Elizabeth, sensitive to the emotional turmoil of the earlier evening, refrained from intruding. The echoes of love lost reverberated in her mind, intensified by the proximity of one of those loved ones just inches away. With each sip of the dark beverage, the atmosphere in the room seemed to undergo a subtle transformation. The quiet, contemplative mood shifted, creating an unspoken undercurrent that mirrored the Elizabeth's internal conflict.

Breaking the silence, Elizabeth whispered, "George, can you hold me?" His gaze shifted towards her, emerging from the depths of his thoughts. It took a moment for him to register her request. Initially hesitant, he noted the exposed vulnerability on her face, realizing that, in that moment, she sought a physical connection more than anything else in the world.

George recalled observing Elizabeth's compassionate interaction with the girls earlier in the evening. He experienced a twinge of regret for not being able to offer her the emotional support she really sought. The intimate, loving, romantic relationship between a man and a woman. There was too much complexity in their shared history. However, he had to acknowledge the unspoken bonds that tied them together.

George adjusted his position, making room for her to slide over and settle beside him. He encircled her with his arm as she rested her head on his shoulder. They continued in companionable silence for a while before Elizabeth spoke again.

"I love you, George. I always have," she whispered.

George cleared his throat, pulling her closer. "I know," he replied simply. The unspoken weight of their shared history hung in the air, and the simplicity of George's acknowledgment hinted at a depth of understanding between them.

"Why didn't you choose me?" she whispered, almost to herself. The words slipped from her lips, not intended for George to catch a glimpse of the tumultuous thoughts within her. However, it jolted her when George responded.

As he embarked on articulating his response, he sensed her tensing, a subtle indication of her inclination to withdraw. Undeterred, he tightened his embrace, keeping her securely close. There was a necessity to convey the complexities of his emotions in a way that resonated with her. He sought to unravel the truth behind her question now that she had mustered the courage to ask.

"We had grown up together, faced the trials of life side by side, yet the choice I made all those years ago still lingers like a shadow between us. In the dance of time, I loved your sister more than you, and circumstances led me to choose your older sister, leaving you on the periphery of our romantic entanglements," George confessed.

In the ensuing quiet, George sensed her body shivering, a delicate attempt to restrain a quiver, a prelude to an impending sob coursing through her. He harbored no desire to inflict pain upon her, yet a compelling need urged him to impart the truth regarding why he could never entertain romantic involvement with her.

In the soft glow of the parlor, the image of Elizabeth remained intertwined with memories of the little girl he once knew. "The innocence of our shared past lingered, creating a bittersweet tableau in my mind. Even now, as you have grown into a woman, I still see traces of that young girl and your older sister in you, and it complicates the dynamics between us."

As he continued to hold her in that quiet moment, the unspoken truths hung heavy in the air. "I couldn't be the emotional anchor you need in a romantic sense," George continued. A sense of regret whispered through the room. The warmth of her presence was undeniable, yet the emotional boundaries he had set in the past limited the depth of the connection he could share in the present.

He continued speaking softly while stroking her shoulder and her hair. "The complexities of our history, the choices made, and the unspoken sentiments forged a delicate tapestry that painted our relationship in hues of nostalgia and longing. I don't want to break that and I can't see the woman sitting here with me now as anything more than the little girl I knew long ago."

Elizabeth fell into a hushed silence, ceasing her futile attempts to extricate herself from George's grasp. Slowly, she settled into the comfort of his shoulder, her eyelids drifting closed. The realization of why he kept her at arm's length lingered, casting a somber shadow over her emotions. Despite the discontent that swirled within her, acceptance became her only recourse.

In the quiet of the night, Elizabeth surrendered to the weariness that enveloped her, succumbing to the embrace of sleep within the circle of George's arms.

"She's asleep now," George mumbled to the walls. "But... this quiet doesn't feel final," he finished. Something in him told him this was far from completed.

Gently, he cradled her form, carrying her up to her room, and tenderly placed her in bed. With a lingering gaze, he left her to the quietude of her dreams before retiring for the night himself.

PENELOPE HARTFORD
"Penny"

10

In the weeks that followed, the Hartford household settled into a quieter rhythm — though not a gentler one. Elizabeth's influence over the home expanded steadily, her opinions on everything from politics to daily life woven into instruction and expectation. What began as guidance soon became routine, and it pressed down on everyone beneath the roof.

Elizabeth sought to try and get more time near George. Her heart was still tied to him. Years after their first meeting, she still loved him. She understood that he'd fallen in love with her sister, married her and had children, but she'd died, just like her husband had died. Elizabeth saw no reason why she couldn't let George know of her interests and so she had. It didn't work out well.

Meanwhile, in the heart of the storm, Penelope's father, George, stood firm in his beliefs. He had been an outspoken critic of British rule, his voice carrying his conviction. This, however, had not escaped the notice of Elizabeth, his sister-in-law. She was a staunch Loyalist, unwavering in her loyalty to the British Crown.

In the dimly lit study, Elizabeth's gaze lingered on George, her eyes betraying the emotions she struggled to conceal. Her heart had long harbored affection for him, a love that had refused to wane despite the years that had passed. His presence in the room, with his convictions and the resolute fire in his eyes, only intensified the longing within her. As the minutes ticked by, she couldn't bear the silence any longer.

"George," she began, her voice quivering ever so slightly. "I believe it's time we talk about what I feel."

He turned his attention to her, his brow furrowing with a mixture of anticipation and apprehension. The gravity of her words hung in the air, and he nodded for her to continue.

"I know it's been many years," she admitted, her eyes never leaving his. "And I know you loved my sister, married her, and had a family. I mourned her passing just as I mourned my husband's." Her voice wavered, betraying the pain that still clung to her heart. "But, George, my feelings for you haven't changed. They've remained constant from since we were children."

As she spoke, George's eyes darted away, his jaw clenched with the emotions that had remained unspoken. He had long suspected the depth of her affection, but he had never dared to confront it. He thought that on the night of the de La Pointierre's departure that he'd let his stance be known to her. Now, in this moment, the inevitability of the conversation being revisited bore down upon him.

Elizabeth, however, refused to let the conversation lapse into silence. "George, are there reasons why you can't love me?" she argued, her voice taking on a fervent tone. "You see me as my sister, don't you? A ghost of the past? It's not fair to either of us. You've placed her on a pedestal, and I've been a mere echo all our lives."

He couldn't find the words to respond. Each of her arguments held a painful truth, a truth he couldn't deny. It was his love for her sister that had bound him, and it was the memory of that love that had kept him from seeing the woman before him. As he looked at her, he realized that he could never give her love beyond that of a sister. She reminded him too much of the little girl he knew from the past, no matter how much more she had developed into a woman.

But as the silence stretched on, he couldn't help but think to himself, '*She may look similar but she is not her sister. She is not my ex-wife.*' The realization was a bitter pill to swallow, for it carried truth. Elizabeth was her own person, just not someone he felt he could fall in love with.

George's refusal to consider a relationship with Elizabeth became a constant source of tension between them. He found her close-minded and disapproved of her actions, especially those that had brought misery to Minuette and Clauvère. George had contemplated sending her away, but he couldn't. She had nowhere else to go and he had a responsibility to take care of her. He loved her, just not romantically. Elizabeth, seething with anger, at his reluctance to love her as a woman, continued to harass him on that point, refusing to give in.

Their conversation was abruptly halted by the entrance of a servant into George's study, urgently beckoning his attention.

"Sir, I hate to interrupt you and the madam, but there are British troops outside who call for your presence," the servant relayed.

George exchanged a perplexed glance with Elizabeth, who mirrored his confusion.

"George," she began, concern etching her features. "Is everything going to be alright? What do you think this is all about?"

Rising from behind his desk, George approached Elizabeth. Placing his hands on her shoulders, he attempted to provide reassurance. "I'm sure it's just a minor matter. I'll go out and ascertain what this is all about," George assured her. Sensing the need for further comfort, he leaned forward, planting a kiss on her forehead.

The British troops had descended upon the Hartford estate and surroundings. Their numbers were unreasonable for their stated purpose but it seemed like the commanding officer wanted to put on a show of force. Not for the Hartford family but for George's neighbors, who were likely already aware of what was going on.

Captain Thomas Haring had decided to take matters into his own hands after hearing the conversation between Elizabeth, Amelia, and Penelope in the market. The conversation itself was harmless — the sort of family disagreement heard in every market square. But it confirmed something Captain Haring already suspected: George Hartford spoke freely, publicly, and without fear. Not a criminal. But a man who could be made into one.

This wasn't about potential troublemakers among the local Whig and Moderate population. He was going to use this opportunity to further his position within the army.

He had decided to turn George into the event that would propel him to Major. George had never been one to keep his opinions under wraps. He believed in the freedom to express his views openly, considering it his inherent right. Unfortunately, his presumption was about to be shattered.

On that fateful day, Captain Haring and his squad of British soldiers formed a formidable line in front of the Hartford mansion, their weapons poised and pointed directly at the house. The air was tense, pregnant with uncertainty. As George neared the front door of the house, he heard a voice ring out.

"George Hartford, step forward. You have inquiries to address," Captain Haring's authoritative voice rang out.

George, bewildered by this unexpected show of force, hurriedly buttoned up his jacket as he stepped onto the expansive porch. "What is the meaning of all this?" he demanded.

The captain's response was stern and accusatory. "You stand accused of sedition against the Crown. You have been branded a rebel, and you shall be brought in for questioning."

Penelope and Amelia inched their way out of the front door, seeking solace in each other's closeness as they ventured toward their father. The menacing presence of the British soldiers sent shivers down their spines, the glint of their leveled rifles tracing every move with unsettling precision.

As George, puzzled and alarmed, gazed around, his daughters clung tightly to him, their arms encircling his waist. The warmth of their embrace offered a reassuring contrast to the chilling atmosphere of uncertainty.

Elizabeth, appearing behind George, took faltering steps towards the group, her voice quivering as she questioned the unfolding scene. "George, what's happening? Can you explain?" Her hands remained clasped tightly over her chest, an unspoken worry etched across her features.

George's frustration and confusion were evident as he turned to face Elizabeth. "You expect answers from me? I am just as clueless as you are." After addressing Elizabeth, he turned towards the man who appeared to be in charge. "Can someone please enlighten us about the purpose of this intrusion?"

Captain Haring wore a malevolent grin as he fixed his gaze upon George, a sense of authority exuding from him. With deliberate intent, he reached into a satchel slung across his shoulder and retrieved a folded piece of parchment. Once unfolded, he began to recite its contents with an air of finality. "George Hartford, you stand accused of seditious acts, of spreading rebellious sentiment amongst the populace, and inciting unrest against the Crown. By the authority of James Wright, the Royal Governor of Georgia, you are hereby to be apprehended and detained for further questioning, pending your confession of these crimes."

As Captain Haring lowered the parchment, his sharp eyes took in George's visible fear and the pallor that had drained the color from Elizabeth's countenance. An unmistakable, malevolent smirk crept across his features, his satisfaction evident.

Amidst this bewildering and oppressive situation, Penny's voice, soft and filled with concern, broke the tension. She peeked from underneath her father's protective arm and inquired, "Father, what's happening? Why are there so many soldiers?"

George, her anchor in this moment of uncertainty, lowered his gaze to her and leaned closer to offer a reassurance that he wasn't sure he could fully believe himself. "It's all right, Penny. This is simply a misunderstanding, and we will get it sorted out soon."

Amelia, who had also been clinging to her father but on the opposite side, couldn't hold back her own apprehensions. Her voice trembled as she inquired, "Father, is this because of the things you've been saying?"

George shifted his attention to Amelia, raising the arm beneath which she sought refuge and gently patting her head. "Don't worry, Amelia. I haven't said anything that should be considered as being against the Crown. I'll accompany these soldiers to understand what this is all about."

However, Elizabeth couldn't contain her distress any longer, and her voice rang out, her hand outstretched toward George, her words laden with desperation. "No!"

George shifted his stance so that he could meet Elizabeth's gaze. His demeanor remained composed despite the unfolding turmoil. "Take the girls and go inside," he instructed, his voice steady.

Penny, however, resisted, her grasp on her father unyielding, and she pleaded with him. She was determined not to be separated from him, fear and concern etched into her features.

Elizabeth approached in an attempt to extricate the determined girl from her father's side, but she found herself struggling with the task. In her moment of need, she turned toward the door, where Homily had discreetly arrived. She sought Homily's assistance in prying Penny away from her father's protective hold. "Homily, help me here, will you."

Homily stepped forward as she was requested. She proceeded to help Elizabeth in her struggle to free George from Penny's clutching hands. The girl latched onto Elizabeth when she was finally separated from her father. Her face buried in her aunt's dress. Amelia walked over to her aunt and grasped a portion of her dress from the other side. Elizabeth tried her best to comfort the girls to no avail.

Amelia and Penny clung to Elizabeth, with Homily silently standing just behind them. They watched with heavy hearts as George reluctantly left the porch and approached the waiting soldiers. It was a scene laden with foreboding. The soldiers wasted no time; they placed George in handcuffs and began to lead him away.

The consequences were swift and unforgiving. George was taken into custody by British troops, branded as a rebel. This abrupt and unjust act left Penelope devastated, her heart aching for her father. He, a man of unwavering conviction, now found himself confined within the cold, dark walls of a prison, accused of treason and sedition.

This series of events left Elizabeth wavering in her convictions towards the Crown and unsure of what the outcome of this would be. Her heart ached as her desire to run to the man that she loved battled against her knowledge that doing so would accomplish nothing. She looked down at the two girls clutching desperately to her and knew that she needed to be there for them during this time.

Every evening, Penny made a point of bringing her father a meal. Her father, George, appreciated the gesture, finding solace in the warmth of her company. Elizabeth, her aunt, allowed these visits but insisted that Homily accompany Penny. Penny saw it as a small reprieve from her aunt's strict regime, a chance to escape the rigid routine of the household. In gratitude, she gave Elizabeth a heartfelt hug. Elizabeth, ever composed, returned the gesture with a simple embrace. She watched with a detached air as Penny and Homily left the house, carrying a basket filled with food, and boarded the waiting carriage.

Amelia had chosen not to go with them that evening. She told herself it was only for this visit, that she needed a little distance before everything overwhelmed her. Even so, the decision did not sit easily. As the carriage pulled away, guilt followed close behind, whispering that she had abandoned her sister when she should have been there. She felt, briefly, as though she had failed in some small but important way. Yet she also knew that Penny would not see it as a failure. Penny never asked for more than someone could give, and Amelia tried to take comfort in that, even if it did not entirely quiet her unease.

The carriage ride, however, lacked excitement. The world around them continued to spin, seemingly indifferent to the turmoil that had befallen their family. It was as though their personal tragedy had temporarily put their lives on hold, while the rest of the world carried on with its business.

The carriage rumbled along the cobblestone streets, and Penny sat quietly, gazing out the window. The evening sun painted the sky in warm hues, but her thoughts were far from the picturesque scenery passing by.

Homily, sitting beside Penny, noticed her distant expression. She reached out and gently touched Penny's hand, her voice soft and caring. "Penny?" When Penny turned to look at her, Homily continued, "Do you miss him?"

Penny's brow furrowed in confusion for a moment, but then it cleared as she realized who Homily meant. "Oh, you mean Chevalier Clauvère?" She couldn't help but smile at the thought of him.

Homily nodded, her eyes filled with curiosity. "Yes, Miss Penny, Chevalier Clauvère. Do you miss him?"

Penny turned her gaze back to the passing scenery, her smile lingering. "Every day," she admitted. "He's the most handsome man I've ever met, and he's kind, and he believes in things that matter." Her voice grew wistful as she added, "I can't help but think about the future, about what it would be like to be with him."

Homily listened intently, her heart heavy with unspoken emotions. She had watched the blossoming romance between Penny and Clauvère, and she couldn't help but feel a twinge of sadness. "You two make a lovely couple," she said, her voice tinged with longing.

Penny's smile faded, and she turned to Homily, seeing the sadness in her eyes. "Homily, what's wrong? You deserve love and happiness too."

Homily sighed softly, her gaze still fixed on the passing scenery. "I wish, Miss Penny. I wish I could have a love like yours. But sometimes, life has different plans for people like me."

Penny reached out and took Homily's hand in her own, offering comfort. "Don't say that. You're kind, caring, and wonderful. Love has a funny way of finding people when they least expect it."

Homily's eyes welled up with tears, and she squeezed Penny's hand in gratitude. "Thank you, Miss Penny. Your words mean the world to me."

As the carriage continued its journey, Penny and Homily shared a moment of silent understanding. While they both yearned for love in their lives, they also knew that the future was uncertain. But as long as they had each other, they could face whatever challenges lay ahead with hope in their hearts.

Shortly after Penny and Homily's heart-to-heart conversation, the carriage came to a halt in front of Peter's home. Peter, a close acquaintance, was required to accompany Penny when she ventured outside. Elizabeth, recognizing her staffing shortage at home, had reluctantly called upon Peter's assistance. It was a decision made out of necessity rather than personal preference because Peter was quite young too.

As Peter entered the carriage and took his seat across from Penny and Homily, he couldn't help but notice Homily's subtle reaction. A faint blush graced her cheeks, though it was difficult to discern due to the color of her skin. However, her tendency to avoid eye contact with Peter, a tousle-haired young white boy, was unmistakable.

Peter, ever observant, had picked up on Homily's discomfort from the very first day they had started the routine of delivering food to Penny's father. In a playful manner, he decided to gently tease her, hoping to alleviate some of her unease.

"You look rather pretty tonight," Peter commented, a mischievous glint in his eye. He turned towards the carriage window and drew the shades open with a theatrical flair. "The moonlight outside pales in comparison to your radiance."

Homily found herself squirming in her seat, her unease evident. She tightly clutched Penny's nearest arm with both of her hands and leaned in closer to her. In a barely audible whisper, she responded, "Thank you."

Peter continued his light-hearted teasing, sensing Homily's discomfort but not intending any harm. He leaned in closer, maintaining his playful tone. "You really should consider wearing dresses like that more often, Homily. You have a certain elegance about you, and I think you look stunning in them."

Homily had adorned herself in a simple yet elegant dress, a departure from the usual maid's outfit she typically wore around the house. This particular garment was one of a half dozen dresses Penelope had acquired for her over the years. Despite being grateful for the gifts, Homily initially resisted, deeming herself too low in status to wear such finery. However, upon Penelope's persistent insistence, she eventually relented.

Homily shifted nervously, casting a quick glance at Penny who was growing increasingly concerned about her friend's unease. Peter's good-natured teasing had taken an uncomfortable turn, and she couldn't stand to see Homily squirm in discomfort any longer.

"Peter," she interjected, her tone gentle yet firm, "I think you've had your fun. Let's not make Homily more uncomfortable."

Peter, recognizing Penny's concern, immediately stopped his teasing and nodded in agreement. "You're right, Penny. I didn't mean to make Homily uncomfortable. I'm sorry." He turned to Homily. "Look, Homily. I meant what I said. You look beautiful in that dress and I'm sorry if it seemed like I was making fun of you," he offered with a smile.

Homily, grateful for Penny's intervention, managed a relieved smile, her unease finally fading. Penny, Peter, and Homily settled into a more relaxed atmosphere for the remainder of the ride, their conversation turning to more neutral topics, and the moonlight outside casting a gentle glow on the carriage.

As the carriage carried Penny, Peter, and Homily toward the British garrison, the atmosphere grew heavy with anticipation. The evening had cast a dusky shroud over the city of Savannah, but in the distance, the British garrison glowed like a beacon of authority. The lantern lights from the windows flickered warmly, illuminating the stern exterior of the colonial stronghold.

The garrison was an imposing structure, its walls standing tall and unyielding in the dim light of evening. The windows, adorned with lanterns, emitted a golden glow, revealing a glimpse of life within its stern walls. Soldiers in their scarlet coats moved with military precision, their presence a stark reminder of the ever-watchful British presence in the colonies.

Homily, sitting beside Penny, cast furtive glances at the garrison, her apprehension palpable. The sight of the soldiers and the garrison always made her uneasy, a reminder of the challenges faced by those who sought to challenge British authority. Peter, sensing her discomfort, reached out and placed a reassuring hand on Homily's shoulder, offering her a small, supportive smile.

Penny, too, was contemplative. The garrison symbolized the very power that had taken her father from her, yet it was also the place she needed to visit to ensure his well-being. Her thoughts were a mixture of apprehension and determination, her gaze focused on the lantern-lit windows that held the answers she sought.

As the carriage drew nearer to the garrison, the lantern lights appeared more vivid, casting dancing shadows on the cobblestone path. The trio continued their journey, the glow of the lanterns growing stronger with each passing moment, an eerie and constant reminder of the British presence and the mysteries that awaited them within the formidable walls.

In the shadows of those harsh walls, Penelope visited her father as often as she could, her young heart heavy with worry and her eyes brimming with tears. The trio received permission to visit her father, and as they entered the cold and forbidding prison, it was clear that George welcomed the presence of others who were not bound by shackles and confined behind the unforgiving iron bars that caged him.

George, with the heavy iron bars separating him from his youngest daughter, did his best to convey his affection through the restrictive barrier. As they connected in this limited way, Penny couldn't help but notice the striking change in her father's appearance. His figure seemed more gaunt, his complexion pallid, a stark contrast to the robust and healthy father she once knew.

With a wan smile, Penny greeted her father, her heart heavy at the sight of him confined in such deplorable conditions. "Good evening, father," she offered, struggling to find cheer in a situation so bleak and unjust.

Anxiously, she inquired, "What did they tell you, Father? Are there any signs of them releasing you soon?"

George, realizing the inevitability of his fate, made a heart-wrenching decision. He spoke the truth to his youngest daughter, Penny, despair in his voice.

"I won't be coming home, Penny. You need to keep away from here. I don't want you to see me like this," he whispered, his voice quivering. He was making a painful sacrifice to protect his youngest daughter from witnessing his grim end.

Penny's eyes widened with disbelief, and her heart sank as her father's words pierced through her like a dagger. She couldn't fathom the enormity of what he was telling her. The thought of her father not returning home, never being able to embrace him, was a heavy burden to bear.

"No, father," she pleaded, her voice trembling with an emotional mix of fear and sadness. "There must be something we can do. We can find help, talk to someone, plead your case. I can't just let you stay here like this. You can't give up."

George's eyes, filled with a profound love for his daughter, met hers. He wished more than anything that he could protect her from the harsh reality he was facing. His voice remained soft, but resolute. "Penny, my dearest, it's not a matter of giving up. It's a matter of ensuring your safety and well-being. This is a fight I can't win. I've made my peace with it, but I can't bear to see you suffer through this with me. You must stay away, promise me."

The heavy decision he had made to protect his beloved daughter was etched on his weary face. Penny, fighting back tears, knew she couldn't change his mind. With a trembling voice and a heavy heart, she nodded in reluctant agreement. "I promise, father, but please know that we'll find a way to make things right. You won't be forgotten."

As they exchanged these painful words, the despair and helplessness hung thick in the air, a father's sacrifice for his daughter's well-being, a poignant moment etched into their shared history.

With great care, both Peter and Homily had to gently pry Penny away from the cold jail bars, her desperate attempts to reach her father breaking their hearts. She appeared dazed, her eyes filled with confusion and sorrow. Peter suspected that shock had overwhelmed her, and he was determined to get her home to safety. Together, they guided her towards the awaiting carriage and set out for the Hartford home.

Meanwhile, George's eyes had followed the children as they left, the untouched food before him a grim reminder of his impending fate. He had no appetite, his situation too heavy to bear. The uneaten meal remained in front of him, as he had not yet revealed to Penny that his execution was scheduled for the morning.

The inevitable fate could not be escaped; George, deemed a traitor to the Crown, was to face the gallows for his convictions. His business had narrowly avoided confiscation, but the specter of its eventual failure loomed in his absence, casting a shadow over his family's future, one defined by a legacy of rebellion.

When she got home, Penny informed her aunt and sister of what George had said. Elizabeth seemed to take the news just as hard as Amelia. Penny's voice trembled as she pleaded with Elizabeth. "You must help, Aunt Elizabeth. Father is innocent! He doesn't deserve this fate."

Elizabeth's unwavering gaze was met by the gravity of her words, her voice barely above a whisper as she voiced her apprehensions, "Penelope, my dear, it is imperative that we align ourselves with the Crown during these tumultuous times. Your father's choices have repercussions, whether we find them palatable or not." Internally, Elizabeth was shaken to the core. She couldn't accept that things had come to this.

Elizabeth's introspective thoughts conveyed the turmoil within her. She had not intended to utter those fateful words publicly in the marketplace, a moment of indiscretion that led to George's arrest. Her journey from England had been driven by the hope of winning George's affection, but now, in the midst of this turmoil, her dreams seemed to crumble. She was plagued by a sense of dread, knowing she would never see George again.

Elizabeth, despite her unknowing implicit role in her brother-in-law's downfall, had assumed control of the family home upon George's arrest. She was acutely aware that Penelope and Amelia were the rightful heirs to the estate, and her newfound mission was to secure their future. However, her methods raised moral questions.

With determination, Elizabeth plotted to keep the girls with her as long as she could, all while exerting control over the estate. Her intentions, regrettably, were far from noble, as she aimed to manipulate the sisters to serve her interests, keeping a remnant of the man she loved next to her as long as she could. She was determined that she would see that the girls remained safely ensconced. If they were to marry eventually, the prospective suitors would need to possess not only the appropriate temperament but also impeccable social standing, with noble lineage as the paramount criteria.

She refused to accept the idea that authority alone granted the right to destroy lives and call it order. She had seen how easily a man without standing could be condemned, how quickly truth bent beneath title and uniform. Never again would she allow that imbalance to leave her nieces exposed.

Amelia and Penelope now faced an impending challenge: arranged marriages and a contentious inheritance, all set against the backdrop of a world forever altered by the Revolution. The path ahead was precarious, and they would have to navigate it skillfully, as their lives were woven into a complex web of change and uncertainty.

Tears welled up in Penelope's eyes, and she watched helplessly as her father's fate hung in the balance. Clauvère's family had departed, and now Penelope's own family faced an agonizing separation.

Weeks had turned into a month after George's initial arrest, up until this point. Controversy raged on within the American colonies and George's situation had grown increasingly dire. His once jovial spirit had dwindled, replaced by the heavy weight of impending doom. He had been sentenced to execution, a fate that haunted the Hartford estate like a ghost.

The next morning was overcast, the Hartford family was dealt a staggering blow when news arrived that George was scheduled to be hanged as punishment on that day. The revelation sent shockwaves through the household, leaving Penny particularly incensed that her father had kept the dreaded day of his execution a secret.

Amelia sat in the parlor, her face ashen with grief, clutching a handkerchief tightly in her hand. Elizabeth's response was more visceral; her despair overwhelmed her, and she fainted as the grim reality sank in.

Elizabeth knew better than to resist. Word had already been sent. Attendance was not optional. In matters of treason, the family was expected—not as mourners, but as witnesses to the Crown's judgment — absence would have been noted, and remembered

The burden of attending to their grief-stricken aunt fell upon the girls. Once Elizabeth regained enough strength to travel, they embarked on the painful journey to the execution site. For her, witnessing George on the gallows was a cruel confirmation that her worst fears had become a heartbreaking reality.

A somber crowd gathered at the town square, where a makeshift gallows had been erected. The town square was filled with onlookers, some in support of the British, others appalled by the unfolding tragedy. As the noose tightened around George's neck, a hushed tension fell over the crowd. The wind whispered through the oak trees, and the town crier's voice carried the moment.

The final moments were excruciatingly slow, the inevitable horror unfolding before the eyes of Penelope and the rest of the Hartford family, the consequences of decisions made in a time of war.

As George's life slipped away, a hollow silence engulfed the square, broken only by the mournful sobs of Penelope, Amelia, Elizabeth, and Homily. The anguished cries of those who had known and loved him. His unjust execution hung heavily in the hearts of those who had witnessed the harrowing event.

In the midst of a country torn by conflict, the Hartford family had endured a grievous loss, their lives forever marked by the choices they had made and the cost they had paid. The impending Revolutionary War had brought not only political change but also the irrevocable transformation of families and their fates.

explicitus est liber

Penelope and Clauvère
As young adults

Also by J. A. Springs

Braiding Fortunes
Braiding Fortunes: A Story of Luck and Bravery of the Heart - Act I Fortune
Woven

Chronicles of Cosmic Realms
Shadows of the Forgotten Void

elctrcsheepdrmwrks (Electric Sheep Dreamworks)
Blurred Vision
Fractured
Zero One

Essays in Systems and Being
Essays in Systems and Being

The Absurdities Anthology
How Not to Find Your Local Weed-Man

The Gifted

The Untamed Force

Next Exit

The Shepherd Series

The Bad Shepherd

The Good Wolf

Standalone

Sundrops

Behind the Red Door

Boundless Fragments: A Collection of Novellas and Short Stories

Fragments of Forever

Somewhere That Isn't There

Watch for more at https://authorjasprings.com.

About the Author

I'm J. A. Springs.

Father of six wonderful children. I served twenty years on active duty, living around the world and experiencing things I never imagined I would. I spent time in societies and countries I once couldn't have envisioned as part of my future. I've done a lot—and still not enough.

These days, I live quietly, accompanied by my cats, music, and an interest in writing that consumes me. I've been writing seriously since 2021. I never set out to write in a particular genre—it made more sense to write around them instead. As for goals? There aren't many. Enjoy the first cup of coffee in the morning and see what the day brings.

Read more at https://authorjasprings.com.

About the Publisher

LLC. Lancaster, PA

www.writingfortheworldpress.com

Read more at https://www.writingfortheworldpress.com.

www.ingramcontent.com/pod-product-compliance
Lightning Source LLC
LaVergne TN
LVHW090946080826
845145LV00003B/904

* 9 7 8 1 9 6 6 4 6 4 2 0 4 *